T0108431

The End of Youth

The End of Youth

Rebecca Brown

City Lights Books
San Francisco

Cover design: Stefan Guttermuth / double-u-gee
Text design and composition: Harvest Graphics
Editor: Robert Sharrard

Library of Congress Cataloging-in-Publication Data

Brown, Rebecca, 1956–
    The end of youth / by Rebecca Brown
       p.   cm
    ISBN 0-87286-418-9 / ISBN 978-0-87286-418-4
I. United States—Social Life and customs—Fiction. 2. Maturation
(Psychology)—Fiction.
3. Life Changes events—Fiction. I. Title.

PS3552.R6973 E5 2003
813'.54—dc21   200204167

CITY LIGHTS BOOKS are edited by Lawrence Ferlinghetti and
Nancy J. Peters and published at the City Lights Bookstore, 261
Columbus Avenue, San Francisco, CA 94133. Visit our Web site:
www.citylights.com

Acknowledgments

Many of the texts in this volume first appeared in other publications and the author thanks the editors of the many magazines, journals, and anthologies for publishing them.

"Heaven" first appeared in an earlier and much abbreviated form in *The Stranger*.

"Learning to See" was first published in *The Bellingham Review*, edited by Brenda Miller.

"Afraid of the Dark" was published by 10th Avenue East Publishing in *The Rendezvous Reader*, edited by Paula Gilovich and Evan Sult.

"The Fish" appeared in a vastly different form in *The Evolution of Darkness* (Brilliance Books).

"Nancy Booth, Wherever You Are" first appeared in *Queer* 13 (Rob Weisbach Books, William Morrow and Company), edited by Cliff Chase.

"A Vision" first appeared in *A Woman Like That* (Bard Books), edited by Joan Larkin.

"The Smokers" was first published in *Conjunctions* 36. Parts of it, though, appeared in an earlier form in *The Stranger*.

"Breath" was first published in *The Raven Chronicles*.

"My Mother's Body" appeared in slightly different form in *Excerpts from a Family Medical Dictionary* (Grey Spider Press, 2001).

"Description of a Struggle" appeared in part in the Bucknell College online journal of new writing, edited by Carla Harryman. The complete text was published in *Gargoyle* 44, edited by Richard Peabody and Lucinda Ebersole.

"Inheritance" appeared in *Monkey Puzzle,* edited by Kreg Hasegawa and Daniel Comiskey.

"There" was published in a limited Xerox format by LD Productions, a Seattle-based magazine.

Thanks to David White for computer expertise, Leo Bassetti for the use of the cabin in the woods, Stokley Towles for editorial assistance, and John Kazanjian of Seattle's New City Theatre for asking for a play. And, as always, Chris.

Contents

Heaven

I've been thinking a lot about heaven lately. I've been trying to imagine it. In one version heaven is a garden, not Eden, but a great, big vegetable garden with patches of zucchini and crookneck and summer squash and lots of heavy tomato vines with beefsteak and cherry and yellow tomatoes getting perfectly, perfectly ripe, and zinnias and cosmos and lots of other flowers. There's an old lady in the garden. It's sunny out and she's wearing blue jeans and a T-shirt. She's healthy and tan and stooping down over one of these plants. Lying half asleep in the sun on the path behind her is a cat and they are happy.

In the other version, heaven is a big field near a lake. It's early in the day, before the sun has risen, and the air is brisk and cool and ducks are flying overhead. There's a guy in the field, a tall, strong guy with the healthy, clean-smelling sweat of someone walking. He's wearing his duck hunting gear, his waders and corduroy hat and pocketed vest. He's moving toward the water's edge where he'll shoot a couple of birds to bring home to his family.

The lady in the first heaven is my mother, brown-skinned and plump, with a full head of hair, the way she was before she turned into the bald, gray-skinned sack of bones she was the month she died. The guy in the second version is my father, clear-eyed and strong and confident, not the sad and volatile, cloudy-eyed drunk he was for his last forty years. I've been thinking about heaven because ever since my parents died I've wished I believed in some place I could imagine them. I wish I could see the way I did when I was young.

Learning to See

When I was born, I had a crooked eye. It was my right eye. It looked straight into my head.

It was often referred to as "the" crooked eye, rather than "her" or "your" eye. It was as if it was not part of me, but something that had attached itself to me. I don't remember how it felt. I do know that it made me feel different.

I was the youngest of three kids. After my sister and brother were born, my parents decided to stop having children. However, several years later, though their marriage was going to hell, they got pregnant again. My mother got this idea that maybe this unexpected baby might be the thing to coax her increasingly wandering husband home. When I was born I looked like him. I had his wavy hair, his coloring, his skinny arms and legs. I also had the blue, blue eyes my mother had fallen in love with.

One of these eyes, however, was crooked. The crooked eye, I'm told, made it uncomfortable to look at me. It was polite, back in the '50s, to look away from things like that. People assumed, because of the lost, half-vacant way I looked and the clumsy way I moved that I was—and this was the word they used back then—"retarded." My family tried to compensate for this. My sister and brother spoke for me. For my first three years I didn't say a word. Instead I listened and in the odd, unbalanced way I could, I looked.

I don't remember what I saw. Did I see only half the world? Was what I saw a part? Did I not have perspective? Did I look more inside myself? Did I see better in?

Soon my mother gave up hope her marriage could be saved; she determined in its stead to save my sight. I know my mother wanted me to be normal. I also know she felt responsible for my eye. The crooked eye was a punishment, a sign that she and her husband had failed at love.

She took me to a specialist, Dr. Blumberg. I remember his name because forever afterward my mother spoke of him with reverential gratitude. He was a quiet, careful man. I remember him lifting me up onto the big, high leather chair in his office and his cool, dry hands that smelled like soap. I remember the cone-shaped thing in front of my face and that I was supposed to look at something on the wall but I couldn't see it.

Dr. Blumberg told my mother that surgery would have too many risks, but exercise might fix the crooked eye. They got me glasses when I was two. I have seen pictures of me in them: the light blue, pointy, plastic frames looked huge on me, like goggles. They also put a patch over my left, good eye, so I couldn't see out of it. This was to force the bad, right, eye to turn. The patch was flesh colored, like a big round Band-Aid. It had that same adhesive too. It fit over my entire eye socket and eyebrows and eyelashes. I could almost open my eye beneath the patch, but whenever I did my lashes got stuck and it hurt to try to close the eye again. My skin itched but I couldn't scratch. The glasses and the patch made the world look suddenly strange. I could see even less of everything and part of what I saw was dark, completely black or, if it was very bright outside, a weird, watery brownish-orange where the light came through the patch. For a while I was afraid to move.

I did the exercises with my mother. We did them with the glasses on and with the glasses off but always with the patch. I'd sit on a chair in front of her and my mother would move a pencil or her index finger left and right and up and down and tell me to follow with my eye.

I remember sitting across from her and wanting to do what she asked. I remember sitting still for long and looking. Doing the exercises was my special time with her. This, not the fact that my vision was supposed to improve, was the reason I loved doing them.

Every few days the bandage was changed. My mother was always careful with this, but when she pulled it off it stung. My skin felt hot and sharp. I remember, one time, looking into the mirror once and seeing the skin around my eye was pale and white inside the circle of red where the patch had stuck.

The patch wasn't like the regular Band-Aids I'd get when I'd fall and skin my knees or get gravel in the palms of my hands or around my fingers where I bit my nails. You could see, when you took off a regular Band-Aid to change it, if a scab was forming or if it was getting infected. But with the eye there was nothing quick to see. It happened slowly.

After a while I graduated from the adhesive patch to a dark red plastic disc that slipped over my left lens. This allowed me to see a little out of the good eye, while keeping the burden on the weak one. My brother and sister thought the red lens looked cool, like a beatnik.

Eventually the crooked eye began to move and I saw more of the outside world.

I did not, however, see less inside of me. When I closed my eyes I still could see the things inside my head.

These things were colors, patterns, moving things. Ribbons, puddles of molten oil, and things that shot like flames. They slid across the insides of my eyes like snakes. They were the places I'd dreamed and thought about though I had never been to. They were the things I wanted but I did not know to ask.

Then I graduated to this opaque gritty, gluey stuff I could partly see through, then to just smudges of Vaseline. My mother put on less and less of the Vaseline until finally both the lenses of my glasses were clear and I could look out at the world with both my eyes. About this time, when I was almost four, I began to talk.

I still wear glasses and sometimes, now, when I'm very tired, my weak eye drifts, but mostly my vision is fine. I have also learned to speak. Sometimes, however, I go around without my glasses because I want to see the world the way it used to look: uneven, blurred and glistening, oddly beautiful.

I want to see—and sometimes can—the world where what is seems enough, a world I thought I saw when I was young.

Afraid of the Dark

When I was young my mother would tuck me in at night. She'd pull the covers up to my chin and kiss me and say good-night. I could smell the milky smell of her breath and the sweet smell of her lipstick and the warm smell of her skin. My mother would tell me to close my eyes and go to sleep and put her cool palm on my forehead. Then I felt the quiet ease of pressure lifting off the bed as she stood to leave the room. As soon as she was at my door, I'd shout my answering, "Good-night, Mom," and add, "You can go ahead and stay outside the door again to make sure I fall asleep." My mother would turn and I would watch her silhouette against the yellow hall light wave good-night to me. She'd close the door halfway and I would hear her carpet-muffled steps fade down the hall.

She didn't stand outside my door until I was asleep, but I wasn't really shouting this for her; I was shouting it for me. My voice sounded big in the quiet room; it sounded like I had courage. I wanted to sound like this because I was afraid of the dark.

I often wanted to ask my mother to search through things before she left, to open the closet and shake the coats and sweaters, to lift the blankets and bedcovers and shine a flashlight under the bed, to open the toy trunk and look behind the bookshelf, but I always decided against this because, as much as I didn't want to find it alone, I didn't want *her* to find it.

Outside my window I could see trees and shrubs and the tall wide wall around the yard. The wall was huge and thick and had bits of jagged glass on it to cut robbers or other people who might try to get in. Sometimes all I could see outside was the white glint of moonlight on the glass. But mostly I could see the walkway, wide and smooth, and on nights with a moon, perfect tiny round stones shining in it. The trees were fir with sharp and fuzzy outlines.

Moonlight poured in on my bed. I lay in the faint blue light and looked. I could see the closet across from the window. When the door was open I could see clothes hanging that looked gray and black and white and sometimes blue. Sometimes I could hear them rustle then I could see something hidden, disguised in there, stiff, hard shoulders and legs and the bottoms of feet. I could see something standing tall and quiet, looking at me, and hats on heads and headdresses going up almost to the ceiling. I wondered if it could see me watching it and when it would come out to get me. Was it waiting for me to fall asleep? How did it know? Was it the way I breathed? Or was there some other way I didn't know? Sometimes I tried to make my breathing sound like sleep to see if I could trick it and make it start from the closet and then I could scream and my mother would come and catch it and get rid of it.

When the closet was closed I couldn't see it, but I was sure it could see me through the slats. I listened for it. I heard it moving very quietly then the closet door opening as it came out to get me.

After my mother left my room, my heart started beating faster. I'd lift my arms out from under the covers and fold my hands together over my neck. This was in case it tried to slash my throat or strangle me before I could try to push it away. I always kept my eyes closed because I believed that no one ever killed sleeping little girls. Perhaps because sleeping little girls slept through everything and couldn't hear or see what happened and therefore could not tell. Ignorance *was* an excuse: It was a sleeping girl's insurance. I'd lie as still and stiff as I could. Then, in case it was being overcautious and wanted to ensure my silence, I would pretend that I was dead. I'd listen to the creaks in the wood, the swishing of my head against the pillow, the scrape of branches on the window, the rustle of the crawlies in the rain gutter, the pops and pings of aluminum cooling down. But to me, my eyes clenched closed, my breathing tight and irregular, all of these sounds were it.

When I woke up from a dream sometimes I would be screaming and my mother would be shaking me awake. But sometimes I would wake alone, my eyes sprung open, my breath caught: it had touched me and my voice was gone. It always took me a long time to see. My eyes were foggy at first and things slid over them. I was cold with sweat and didn't know where I was. When I remembered I'd throw my hands over my throat and hope, heart racing, it hadn't noticed I had woken. I would cry, "Momma! Momma!" and my mother

9

would come and turn on the lights and hold me. I often regretted, as soon as I'd called, that my mother was on her way to my room. I wanted to tell her not to come because it was there and it would get her too. I always half expected to see the scattering of dark gauze wings, the slamming of the closet door, the quick black shadow yanking itself back underneath my bed. Though I never did see it thoroughly, I knew I'd only missed it by an instant.

Many nights I felt I hadn't slept at all, like I had lain awake the whole night listening to my heartbeat, listening to it. Every morning when I awoke, I did so with relief. But my relief was only momentary. It was soon replaced with a weighty sense of self-reprimand because I never woke in the protective pose in which I'd gone to sleep. I awoke on my stomach or curled up with my knees tucked up to my chin. I awoke to sheets and blankets disarrayed. I wondered if this was evidence of a midnight scramble out of which I'd fought my way and then, exhausted, fallen back to sleep and then forgotten. Though I could never be sure this was not the case, I doubted that it was or else why, I asked myself, had it allowed me to live?

Every morning I told myself I must try harder. I must stay stiff and straight the whole, entire night, my hands across my neck because I knew some night I'd meet it face to face and I would need to be prepared.

Every summer I went with my mother to visit her mother in Oklahoma City. We didn't visit the house where my mother grew up and remembered loving, but a smaller house her parents had bought after their first two daughters had moved away from home. By the time I remember going there, my grandfather was dead. My father was away a lot and my older brother and sister worked summer jobs so I went with my mother alone.

I remember when my mother's father died. I was in fifth or sixth grade. It must have been a weekend because it was daytime and I was the only one home with my mother. I was in my brother's room listening to one of his records and my mother came in and turned the music down and said, "Daddy died." I knew she didn't mean my father because none of us called him that anymore. Our mother only ever referred to him now as "your father."

"*Gran*daddy," my mother said, "*Gran*daddy's dead," and I knew she meant her father. She was crying.

I remember feeling strange, almost excited. I had never known anyone who had died and I knew it was an important, dramatic thing. I hadn't known my grandfather well. I'd only ever seen him for a few days in the summers when I'd been small. We didn't see him at all for the four years my father was stationed in Europe.

Almost as soon as I was aware of feeling strange, I was also aware I was not comforting my mother. I felt like part of me wasn't there, like part of me was watching from somewhere else. I'm afraid I might have smiled.

I'm sure my mother went up to Oklahoma City for the funeral though I do not remember her doing so. In any event, none of the rest of us went. If my mother went, she must have gone alone.

After Grandaddy died, my mother's mother lived on in the house alone. My mother always said to me, though never to her mother, she didn't like that house. "It feels so cold," my mother said after her father had died. My mother's mother was formal and stiff, a disapproving Methodist. She was the person my mother was most afraid to tell when my father left. My mother got from hers her sense of shame.

The house where my grandfather died was dark, with bricks that were almost black and thick, wide hedges that eventually grew up around the windows so very little light could ever get in. After my mother's father died, the curtains in the house were always drawn.

My mother remembered the other house, the one where she'd lived when she was young, as big and light and open with a big, wide sunny porch where she played with her sisters.

When we went to see her mother, my mother stayed in her father's room and I stayed in Aunt Harriet's. Harriet was, like me, the youngest child of three, the last one to leave home. She and my mother had always been very close. The bedrooms were cool and gray and smelled of lemon polish and had clean white bedspreads with those little white knobs of thread on them. Harriet's room had a big mirror with a dark brown frame and a window by the driveway. There were bushes in front of the window so you could hear cars driving by outside or idling, but all you could ever see of cars was their headlights against the hedges.

I don't remember ever going in my grandmother's room, but whenever I glanced in, it was always dark.

One night when we were staying there, I was suddenly awake. I sat up in bed and saw my mother coming down the hall to the bathroom. I turned on my light. She had come from her mother's room. I got out of bed and was waiting for her when she came out of the bathroom.

"What's the matter?" I whispered.

She whispered back that her mother had had a nightmare.

My mother told me to go back to bed. I went back to bed and turned out the light but I didn't sleep. Orange light came in from the streetlamp and there was a milky gray triangle of light on the floor by my open door. That light was coming in from my mother's room. I heard my mother get in bed, adjust her pillows, sigh. I heard her glasses click open before she put them on, then her taking up a book. I heard her turning pages for a while then after a while the turning stopped and it was quiet. I knew, from how I'd seen before, the sad, defeated way my mother looked sometimes when she stared at the nothing in front of her.

After a while I heard her turn out the light and the rustle and whup of sheets, then her turning and sighing and later her sleeping breath.

The next evening when she and I were out on the back porch for her cigarette—her mother didn't let her smoke inside—she told me that the night before she had heard her mother cry out in her sleep.

"It woke me up," my mother said as she took a drag. "She was having a nightmare."

I wondered if I had heard it too and that's what had woken me up. "Did she say what it was about?" I asked.

My mother blew out the smoke and shook her head. I didn't know if she didn't know or just didn't want to tell me.

My mother had woken me up from nighmares for years

but we never referred to them afterward. I remember her waking me up and holding me and telling me it was just a dream and it was okay now, it was over. When I was very small, I remember she asked me what they were, then she stopped asking. "It's only a dream," she'd say to me, "it's only a dream and it's over now."

Years later, I woke my mother from nightmares too. Though she may have done so for years, I first became aware that my mother cried in her sleep when I was in junior high. My father had left and my brother and sister had gone away to college. My mother and I moved to a small apartment where my mother's room was across the hall from mine. When I heard my mother cry, I would jump out of bed and rush across the hall to her and turn on her light and hold her and say, "It's over now, it's just a dream, it's over, it's over." My mother's eyes were frantic, her face was splotched. After she saw it was only me, she'd try to brush off how afraid she was. She'd ask me to get her a glass of water and I would. Then when I'd come back and try to sit with her she wouldn't let me. She didn't want me to see her like that. She didn't want me to see she was afraid.

So that night, in her mother's house, when my mother said to me, "She sounds like us," I knew the sound she meant. The sound was the cry of a wounded thing, a thing afraid to speak.

The Fish

I asked my father for a nickel and he gave me one and I gave it to the lady sitting in the chair, she had fat legs, and she gave me a green plastic fishing pole that wobbled like licorice. My father put his hands on my arms to help and I heaved it up. I felt my arms tense and tremble and she said, "Fish! Fish! Fish!" She had blue eyes. She put the nickel in her pocket in her cotton dress with flowers. She had beautiful fat hands. I held onto the pole. I looked up at my father and he said, "Hang on, Punk, I think you got a whopper." My father was a fisherman. We had a picture of him that time in Florida when he caught a twenty-three-pound bass on a twelve-pound line. We kept it in the tub for two days so it would still look fresh when the men from *Field and Stream* and *Bob's Gear and Tackle* came by to take the picture. I had to take a bath in my parents' bedroom but sometimes I went in and looked at that fat, beautiful, dead fish in the tub. There was ice in the tub. I couldn't imagine how cold it was. When I put my hand in it stung like it was hot but then I couldn't feel it at all.

My father wore his hunting coat and waders and beige-gold corduroy cap for the picture. He stood in the front yard. It was the bright part of the day, the time when if he had really gone fishing, he'd have been home for hours and the fish would be cleaned and he would be wearing something else. He stood in the bright front yard and held the fish. He held it by its mouth. The eyes of the fish were silver and black and they stared. They looked wet but also shriveled. I wanted them to close but I knew they couldn't.

My sister's friend, the girl from next door who taught her to smoke, was there too and she and my sister were dancing around because my father was going to be famous. My brother had put on his beige-gold corduroy cap too and was standing around but nobody paid attention to him. The men from *Field and Stream* made my father stand a certain way and said, "Just like that, mister. Yessir, that's right. Hold it. Hold it," and told him to smile and he did and they took the picture.

"Hold it, Punk!" my father said. The pole was heavy and I felt it pull. I stretched my arms and the lady said, "Okay, Honey, you got it," and I pulled the pole and my father took the little bag off the clothespeg and handed it to me and gave the pole back to the lady and said, "Thank you, Ma'am." Then he put his arm around me and we walked a couple steps away and he said, "Well, what'd you get?" He wanted me to say something but I just shrugged. I didn't look up at him. "Aren't you going to open it and see what you got?" "Now?" I said. I wanted to keep it a secret longer and surprise myself with it later. "Of course now," he said. "Don't you want to?" "I thought I might save it," I said. "Oh," he said. Then very enthusiastically, as if he'd thought of it, he said,

"That's a great idea, that's a dandy idea," and squeezed my shoulder. Before we walked any further away I turned around and saw the lady give another fishing pole to a boy and I heard her say, "Fish! Fish!"

The bag was wrinkled. I wanted it to stay smooth. While we walked I pushed in the sides and straightened the front and back and refolded the top down the way my mother did my lunch. I didn't look inside. I didn't want to know, not yet, what was inside, although I also wanted to.

My brother liked the rides the most, the roller coaster and the Whip-Poor-Will and the Missile Chaser. My sister liked the Haunted House and the House of Mirrors and both of them liked the bumper cars. I liked the fishing booth. You could get anything there. You could gets cars or dolls or gum or candy or balloons and the fish knew what you wanted. I wondered how the fish knew. My father told me they just knew. Girls got dolls or purses or colors and boys got cars or guns. The fish were put in the bag on the pole. The fish on the pole weren't real fish, you just called them that. The real fish were the fish that bit the line and left the bag on your line as a present to thank you for the bait which was what you paid the lady the nickel for. I called the present in the bag a fish too though because a fish was what you got when you went fishing.

One place we lived somebody lived across the street who had an aquarium. Sometimes I'd go over and I'd watch it. I learned the names: platties, guppies, algae-eaters, catfish, neons, neon tetras, fantail guppies.

One time I remember two orange platties sliding through the water. They brushed a plant and it waved like a "C" and then like a backward "C." There was a pump bubbling at the back with charcoal and angel hair moving very slightly but it was also like everything was perfectly still, like nothing was moving.

There was one small beautiful angelfish. It was about as big as a quarter and had long black-and-white triangle fins and two strings going down from its lips. It was skinny like a dime from the front but round like a quarter from the side. Its eyes were like bumps on the top of the circle and a bit on either side and I wondered if it saw two or even one or how it saw at all. Each of the eyes looked straight but they didn't look together, like one was crooked like mine had been. Sometimes I looked straight at them and one of the eyes looked back at me.

"You must be hungry after that big fishing expedition," my father said. "You want something to eat?" I didn't say anything. We walked over to some tables. He asked me what I wanted and I didn't say anything. He told me he'd be back in a minute and got in line. He was wearing a Hawaiian shirt and khaki slacks and his hair was in a burr. He was home from the Pacific. I knew he wouldn't be home long. I sat down. On the table was a mess, a couple of french fry boats and paper cups and a tinfoil ashtray and some greasy pieces of paper and crumpled napkins. The table was white, round-topped metal and some of the paint was peeling. I could see the rust beneath it, red and brown and crumbling but also wet. I put my little bag in my lap and moved the messy paper and cups to one side and with one of the least ketchupy napkins wiped off the rest of the table, especially the place in front of me and the place opposite me where I knew my father would sit. When it was as clean as I could get it, I put the napkins in the trash pile but I did not take it to the trash can. There was one nearby but one time when I had come with my mother and she had gone to the line and looked back at the table and not seen me there because I was throwing away the trash, she panicked and ran around to find me and told me when she told me to sit I shouldn't go so I sat there and waited for my father. When I had cleaned the table as much as I could, I brought the little bag up from my lap and put it on the table. I recreased the lines of the sides and top. I didn't want to know what was in it right then, I just wanted it like it was, when it could still be anything.

My father returned. He pushed the pile of garbage over to the opposite side of the table where I had thought he'd sit and sat down next to me. He had a large Coke, a hot dog with onions, mustard, and relish, which I could smell, and napkins and a big yellow plastic dish of chocolate ice cream and two plastic spoons. He sat down and started eating the hot dog. I looked at the bag. I heard him take a big slurp of his drink. It sounded like my brother when he was trying to bug my mother. I looked up. My father was grinning. "I got two straws," he said, "and . . ." he slipped them out of the pocket of his Hawaiian shirt and flew them around in the air above the ice cream, "*two*, count 'em, *two* spoons." He took another bite of his hot dog. The cracks in the top of where they scoop it were melting together. The bottom of the dish was starting to get a moat around it from the melting. "You gonna get to work on that while I work on this hot dog?" he asked. He held the spoons out to me, both of them at the same time, between different fingers. I took one and started to eat. My favorite flavor was chocolate.

One time when we moved, my mother got me an aquarium, a ten-gallon one, and we set it up. First you rinse the stones. We got natural-colored ones not the bright fake-looking pink and lime and blue ones. I rinsed them in the sink in a plastic tub. My mother helped. Actually, she did most of it but said I was the one who was doing it and she was only helping. I ran water over the stones and tipped the tub back and forth then poured off the dirt. We washed out the aquarium, wiped it with Windex and paper towels and put the rocks in the bottom. I smoothed them, with more in the back. Then we put water in and let it sit with dechlorinator until it got to be room temperature then we got plants. We brought them home in plastic bags and planted them in the rocks. We got a pump that had angel hair and charcoal. Then we got the fish.

At first we only got a few, a catfish for the bottom and two algae-eaters and two spotted orange platties.

The aquarium was on the kitchen counter near a window. I fed them fish food twice a day. The food was flakes from a plastic can that floated in the water. The fish came up to get it. They put their mouths up to the edge to eat. It looked like breathing. When the food sank they swam down to it. We got more fish, two fantail guppies. The male one had a long beautiful purple and blue and black tail. After a while they had babies. My mother and I put the babies into instant coffee jars, mayonnaise jars, pickle jars. Sometimes the adults ate the babies so we got a thing to put pregnant guppies in and the babies fell through this hole into another jar so no one could eat them. Sometimes when the mother guppies had their babies they just shot out like splinters.

I took the fish to school. At first everyone liked them but after a while there were so many no one else wanted them so I had to bring them back home. Then we separated the mother guppies in the aquarium from the father guppies in jars.

One time my father came home and said, "What's all this?" and I told him we got an aquarium and they were all having babies. "Swell," he said, "just like the goddamn Catholics."

I liked to watch the fish. I'd watch them swim or not swim, sometimes not even move just be there in the water. Sometimes they hid in the plants or behind rocks but I knew they were there.

I wondered why they didn't wrinkle the way my skin did when I stayed in the bath too long. Maybe it was the dechlorinator. I decided to do an experiment. I put my hand in and was going to leave it as long as it would take it to get wrinkled if it was in the bath. When I put my hand in it was cold. I couldn't believe it was room temperature even though the thermometer said 70 degrees.

When I put my hand in it looked greenish-white and crooked as if it had bent. It also looked like it was swaying because of how it stirred the water up. I opened and closed my fist and felt the water. The plants swayed and the fish hid in the plants.

I pushed my fingertips up against the glass and they got white and looked like octopus suckers but when I took my hand away it looked almost normal.

I liked how the water felt on my hand. It felt like nothing out in the air could get to it. The water felt cool and smooth and clean. It felt like swimming only still but in swimming you have to come up to breathe and like this my hand could stay for as long as I wanted.

I kept my hand there very still and after a while the fish started coming out again. They weren't afraid of me.

When I was fourteen I went to see my father. He had moved and I hadn't seen him for a while. He sent me a ticket. My mother hated that I went. I remember waiting to get off the plane. I was standing behind a big businessman in cowboy boots who was taking his time in the aisle like he had all the time in the world. I followed him out of the plane and onto the corrugated steps they'd rolled up to it. It was a small airport. It was windy and the wind whipped my hair and it got caught in my glasses. I waited for the guy ahead of me to go down a few steps. I remember putting my hand over my eyes to keep out the glare as I looked for my father.

I followed the business guy into the lobby and stood behind him while a woman checked our tickets and let us through to the corridor. He walked away ahead of me and I stood by myself. My shoulder bag was heavy. I was carrying too much stuff. I had brought lots of stuff because I couldn't imagine what I would do there besides read. My father had sent me the bag for Christmas a few years ago and I had thought it would be polite to bring it. I had never carried it before.

"Hey, Punk," I heard him say. He was embracing me. I felt his prickly chin against my face and I could smell his smell of aftershave and cigarettes and breath mints. When he let go I saw Mutt, this dog I used to have. Her name had been Sparky but my father never called her that, always Mutt, so that became her name. The dog was jumping around. My father said she remembered me then he introduced me to his new wife. She had on pink nylon stretch shorts and a pink-and-white tank top. I had on a Beatles T-shirt and jeans. I could see her bra strap on her shoulder and when she turned around I could see the dent her bra made in her back beneath the tank top. She was wearing sunglasses and her makeup was caking in the heat.

"Punk, meet Jolene. Jolene, meet Punk."

"Hi Punk," she said, "It's so good to meet you." She sounded like she meant it, slightly nervous. No one else besides my father had ever called me that.

"Pleased to meet you, too," I said. I put out my hand to shake but she reached her whole body toward me to hug me. She was trying very hard. I wanted to try too.

At their house they had our couch and our TV and our dining room table and other things.

I stayed about a week. We went to the beach and out to lunch and we stayed at home and cooked and ate and drank. My father taught me how to mix drinks—highballs and screwdrivers and brandy alexanders and pink ladies and side-cars and Manhattans and margaritas. One time we had a huge Mexican dinner. It took us two days to make and we ate tamales and drank shots of tequila and margaritas and Carta Blanca until we almost got sick. Then we watched the late-night movie and drank brandy alexanders. The movie was about World War II.

I left the room to go to the bathroom. When I came back

it was an advertisement and my father was telling Jolene a story about some great thing he'd done in the war. It sounded like a good story, very heroic and so forth. I heard only the end of it, but that was enough. Then the movie came back on and we watched it again but I looked over at my father. After a while he looked at me. I gave him this look, just kept looking at him. I wanted him to know I knew he was lying. He looked back at the movie. I kept looking at him, knowing he felt me doing so.

The next time there was a commercial Jolene said, "So who's ready for another round?" My father said he was and I said, "Yeah, let's party!" I said it fake cheery. I knew she wouldn't hear it in my voice but that my father would. "Okie-dokie," she said and and went to the kitchen to get more drinks and a fresh pack of cigarettes. Then my father and I were in the living room alone.

"Gosh, Dad," I said with that thing in my voice. "That's not a story I've heard before."

My father kept looking at the ad. Then he said very slowly, "Perhaps you've forgotten it." His voice had that thing too.

"Oh, no," I said, still talking like that, "I'd have remembered that one. That's a really good one. Very dramatic."

I heard my father take a deep breath. I watched his shoulders rise. He was breathing deeply but very quietly so no one else could hear.

"Jolene seems to find your stories . . . enjoyable," I said.

"Stop it," he said. "Stop it right now."

I took a second then I shot up out of my chair and stood at attention and said, the way I'd seen my brother do that one time with our father, "Sir! Yes Sir!"

My father started up from his chair but Jolene was coming back from the kitchen and he made himself sit back down. I took a drink off her tray. When she went to give my father a drink I turned to leave. My father muted the TV and said very firmly, "Don't think you're just going to walk out on me when I'm talking to you."

I stopped but I didn't turn around. My back was to him.

"Turn around and look at me," he said.

I could hear Jolene taking a drink off the tray. I heard somebody drink.

"Look at me," he said again.

I didn't move.

Then he said very, very slowly the way that scared me most, "Look—at—me."

I turned around. I was looking at the floor but I could feel his eyes on me so I had to look up. He stubbed out his cigarette and was looking at me but the next thing he said was to Jolene. "My daughter and I are going to have a little talk. We would appreciate a little privacy."

Jolene stood there a second before she got it. "Oh, okay . . ." she said. "Well I guess it's time for me to toodle off to bed." I watched her leave the room. I felt this flash of something when she was gone. I was suddenly sweaty.

After she left my father settled back in his chair. "I don't know which of her little stories your mother has told you about me but let me tell you the military supported me— and I supported you and don't you goddamn forget it—for years. I believed in defending this country and I still do. And if you don't like it . . ."

"I'm sorry, Dad," I said. But I knew I didn't sound like it.

"I risked my life for you, for all of you, including your goddamned mother, and this is how I'm thanked?"

I felt like a statue. I stared at him. I felt like if he hit me I wouldn't fall down like you're supposed to, I would just stand there like the side of a house or if he hit me hard enough, like with a crowbar, I would splinter apart.

Then he said quietly, like a line from some old movie, "I risked my life for you . . ."

Everything was quiet. I could hear the bugs flying into the light outside on the porch. I could hear his new wife already snoring in the bedroom. I bet she had just fallen on the bed in her clothes.

"That's bullshit, Dad. It's crap. Do you think I don't know why you were piped over? Even the military didn't want you. You were never a fucking war hero. The war was over by the time you got in. This shit about you risking your fucking life—come on. I don't care what great fucking war stories you tell Jolene, but I know it's all a load of crap."

My father's face was red and he was breathing hard. I looked down at the dog sitting at his feet. It was still asleep. When I heard my father shift in his chair, I ran for the door.

I ran from the house to the empty lot across the road. I walked into the middle of it. The night was warm and there was a breeze and I could almost smell the ocean. It smelled salty and clean. The lot was full of weeds. They were grasses as high as my hip and when I walked they swayed. They were gold and beige and silvery in the moonlight and they looked beautiful. I ran my hands along the tops of them, the feathery, seedy husks. The air was dark but clear. I looked back into my father's house.

The front door was open. Pale light was spilling from the house to the porch and yard. The porch light was on, a yellow bulb, and I could see, in the haze around it, bugs flying into it.

I could see a shadow of my father standing. His hands were at his sides. His head was down. His shoulders were bent. I didn't hear anything.

I squatted in the weeds as if I could hide.

I heard my father whistle for the dog. I heard her chains rattle as she jumped around for him to get the leash. They came out to the porch and my father called for me. His voice was tentative. I saw him looking for me but he couldn't see me.

They walked through the yard then across the road to the field. They stood on the edge of it for a while. The dog started jumping around and I ducked down further. My father called for me. He didn't call me Punk; he called my name. The dog was whining. My father undid the dog from the leash and she ran to me and my father came after her. The light from the house was behind him. I saw him coming toward me, bigger the closer he got to me. I heard him pushing the grass aside then he was there. The dog was trying to lick me. I pushed her away and stood up and walked away from them. After a while, I heard them following me.

I had nowhere else to go so I went back to my father's house.

The front door still was open. My father came in behind me. I sat down in front of the TV. It was still on mute and I didn't turn on the sound. The dog came in and sat at my feet and my father went into the bathroom. I heard the water

27

going and when he came out he handed me some Kleenex. I didn't take them from him so he put them on the table and walked away. After he walked away I picked them up and used them.

After a while my father came back and squatted down near my chair and patted the dog and asked, "Want to go for a drive?" He was looking at the dog. I didn't say anything. He patted the dog some more then stood up and looked at me and said, "You want to?" He sounded like a kid.

He went to the kitchen and the dog went with him. I heard him messing around, opening cabinets and drawers and the refrigerator. I heard the dog's nails clicking on the kitchen floor because she was dancing around. She was excited.

When my father came out of the kitchen he had a big brown paper bag. He looked like a boy who didn't know what to say.

I said, "What's in the bag?" and he said, "Bait."

I took the dog and we went to the car. Outside was just the moon and stars. The sky was very clear.

My father loaded the rods and reels and buckets and nets and tackle box in the car. I watched him go from the car to the house. The way he moved, when I couldn't see who he really was, reminded me of my brother.

When he started the car the dash lit up and I could see his hands in the red and green lights. He put it in gear and punched in the cigarette lighter. I looked in the rearview mirror and saw the dog lay down in the back. She put her head on her outstretched paws and closed her eyes.

It was very late and there were only a few other cars on the road. We drove out of town. We rolled down the windows and the air came in. It was warm and I could smell the water and salt. It all smelled clean.

I looked in the rearview mirror and saw the yellow-orange lights of town. I turned around and looked at them out of the back of the window. My father said, "Pretty, huh?" and I nodded.

I turned back around and saw the yellow road divider line in front of us.

When I was little I had imagined it was a chopped-up snake and that as we went along the snake was sliding up into the car and the car was eating it up and one time I asked my father, "When is the trunk going to get full?" He said, "What?" and I told him about the snakes. My father didn't miss a beat. "Oh yeah," he said casually, "I guess I forgot to tell you. There's a new system and the snakes just sleep in the trunk one night and then they get out of the trunk really early in the morning when we're asleep and go back to the road before the morning traffic. It's because there's so many new roads and not enough snakes any more for them to spend as much time in the trunks as they used to. They only get to sleep in there one night at a time." "Oh," I said. I wished that some time I could wake up early enough, like when my father went out to hunt or fish, so that I could see the yellow snakes sliding out of peoples' trunks like noodles to make it back to the road before the morning traffic.

Everything looked greenish white beneath the head-lights and the streetlights. My father turned on the radio. He punched around but there were just late night talk shows and preachers so he turned it off and started to hum like he was about to sing but as soon as he started he stopped self-consciously and changed to whistling. I had only ever heard my father singing once. It was at one of my brother's baseball games when he pitched for the junior high school all stars ("hell of an arm," my father used to say) and there was a big district game and my father came back for it. The game started with "The Star Spangled Banner" so my father sang. My father's singing voice was tentative but he sang every word and kept his hand above his heart through the entire song.

We crossed the bridge that went over to the island then drove off the road and parked on this chalky, rocky place. The car lights shone on the white rocks, a perfect triangle of light that fuzzed out at the edges. When we got out of the car I looked up at the moon. The telephone wires above us looked like tracks across the moon. My father lit a cigarette. The flame leapt up from his lighter then went out and there was just the nub of orange a couple of inches from his face.

We walked to the edge of the water. We set up near beneath the bridge. My father carried the rods and reels and net. I had the tackle box and the brown paper bag of bait and bucket. We set the stuff on the ground then we sat down. The dog sat down behind us, quiet and calm. I put my feet out over the edge. They didn't reach the water. My father leaned over with the bucket and filled it halfway up with water then set it on the ground between us. He got a flashlight from the tackle box and turned it on. I held it while he put the lures on the lines and baited them.

I watched his hands beneath the light. His skin was brown and rough from being outside. His arms were hairy. He wore a flexy wristwatch and I remembered that I had wondered, when I'd been young, how he could wear it without it pinching the hair on his arms. His hands were bony and I could see the thick blue veins beneath the skin. My hands are like that too.

The bait was shrimp. The day before we'd bought it very cheap from someone's boat and got so many we couldn't eat them all but they were so cheap you didn't feel like it was a waste to use them for bait. He took the bait out of the bag and put it on the hook. He said it'd be better if we had live bait but I was glad we didn't because I hated the thought of stabbing things, even worms, on those hooks. I'd always been like that and once when I was little he had told me that fish and worms, any of those kinds of things, don't feel much, they didn't hurt when you had to kill them, but I still felt bad about it.

He fixed the lines and stood up to cast one out. He told me to stay down. I was down already—my father was just being careful. He twisted his upper body, flexed his knees a couple of inches, and slowly moved his right arm behind him. On the top of his arm I could see a line of the light from the moon. Then—whup!—he spun and flung the line out over the water. I couldn't see where it went but I knew it was far. I looked out over the points of the waves that were catching the light of the moon. There was a long skinny triangle of light coming from far out in the water to us. That light washed over us.

My father leaned down and handed the first rod and reel to me then he flung out the second line. The reel unwound more quickly than I could see. When the lure sank he sat on the ground beside me.

We sat beside each other and didn't speak. I felt the rod and reel bob gently in my hand. I watched the red and green lights of a boat going by and the movement of the moonlight on the waves. I listened to the lap of the waves, the eager suck when it reached then fell away from the edge of the land. I could smell the water, a salty smell.

I thought I felt a tug on my line. "Dad," I whispered.

"You got something?"

"I'm not sure," I said.

"Well, bring her in if you think you got something."

I started winding in on the reel. I felt my arms tense up. I was alright until I felt a really hard tug. My father saw this and put his rod and reel down, braced it with a stone, and scooted over to me. The dog started to move and he said, "Hey!" very crisply and the dog sat down and was quiet. I started to hand the rod and reel to him but he said, "You can handle this."

He scooted behind me and put his arms around my shoulders and his hands on the rod and reel over mine. He started winding. "Jesus Christ," he said, "you've really got something here." He moved his hands so I could finish bringing it in.

I saw the line quiver over the water. When the tugging got more difficult—it was only a couple of feet from us—I saw the flash of something struggling. It was the fish.

My father stood. I slipped from between his arms and he lifted the fish from the water and dropped it on the concrete. It flopped back and forth like a spring. My father grabbed the net and scooped it up. He lowered the net and rod to the ground. I watched the fish twisting over and over. I thought of the sand against its oily skin, the stones against its back.

My father leaned over and took the line. I heard a slick noise of the struggling fish. He cupped his hand and lowered it over the fish's mouth. He was careful to miss the hook and fins. He held the fish tightly and twisted the hook from its mouth then quickly went to the bucket and dropped in the fish. The fish swam frantically in circles. It swam for what seemed a long time, then it slowed and finally stopped.

"Quite the little fighter," my father laughed. He put his hand on my shoulder and squeezed it awkwardly, "You got yourself a beaut there, Punk."

"Yeah," I said, "I guess. Thanks."

"Don't thank me," he said, "You did all the work."

"Thanks, Dad," I tried to tell him, "Really. Thank you."

"You bet," he smiled awkwardly and slapped me on the back.

I knew he didn't know what I wanted to say. I squatted down by the bucket and looked at the fish.

"How's about we fry that little beaut up for breakfast?" he said. He sounded happy. "How 'bout it? Just you and me."

I didn't say anything.

"How about it?" he said again a little tentatively. "Fish for two. Not even the damn dog!" He tried to laugh like this was a great joke. The dog got excited and started up again but he clicked his fingers at her and she sat.

I looked at my father squatting over the bucket like some boy my brother might have known. He was waiting for me to say something.

The fish wasn't swimming anymore, it was just sitting there breathing raggedly in the bucket. Its silvery sides went in and out. I couldn't tell if it was slowing down, like relaxing, or if it was dying.

I said, "Can we throw it back?"

My father said, "What?"

"Can we throw it back?" I said again. I couldn't see it moving. I wondered if it was dead. "Can we throw back the fish?"

He looked at me for a second, puzzled, and asked me, "Why?"

I looked out at the water we had pulled it from.

He said, "I mean, we're fishing. Don't you want to get fish? I mean, what are we doing here if we're not fishing?"

I thought I might see blood from its mouth but I didn't. My father had been very careful removing the hook.

"What do you want?" he asked. I could hear in his voice that he was actually asking me something, not just trying to tell me something backward.

"I don't know," I said, "We could just . . . We can fish if you want, I just want to throw it back." I didn't know what I wanted.

My father looked away from me and said, "When I go fishing with other people I don't throw them back."

"I know, Dad," I said. Then, "We don't have to tell anyone else we threw it back. I won't tell. I won't tell Jolene." I wanted to tell him something else. "I won't tell her, Dad. Really. I won't tell her anything."

My father picked up a rod and reel and started fiddling with the line then put it down. He took his Camels from his shirt pocket, shook one out into his mouth and lit it with his squadron lighter. It had an insignia from the carrier he was on that had been too late for the war. He lit the cigarette and sucked in his cheeks and held in the smoke awhile then, after he let it out, said, "Anything?"

"Nothing, Dad," I said, "I won't tell her anything."

He took another drag and looked as if he was going to say something else but he didn't.

Everything smelled alive and wet and salty. I could also smell a slightly rotting smell and knew that if it was day I would be able to see parts of dead fish and crab legs all over where people had partly cleaned them before they put them in the car and took them home. Dogs loved rolling around in them and then the dogs smelled horrible. But my father had trained his dog not to get into them. She was just sitting there, quiet and waiting.

My father went over and looked at the fish. It was moving around again in a circle very slowly. My father kept his cigarette in his mouth as he picked up the bucket with one hand. Then with his free hand he reached for mine and I gave it to him and we walked together to the water's edge. My father put the bucket down and dropped my hand and put his hands in the bucket and caught the fish. He lifted it out and it squirmed. The fish splashed water on me and him.

My father stood up straight and tall and dropped one hand loose from the fish. He arched his right arm behind him and held it a second then he swung out his arm and released the fish.

Before it fell back into the water, there was a moment when it held, the good white fish, shining in space.

Nancy Booth, Wherever You Are

Every year when I was a kid, I went to summer camp. A few times, around the years of my parents' divorce, it was church camp, but most of the time it was Girl Scout camp, which I preferred. At church camp there were boys and girls and boy and girl counselors too. The counselors were earnest football guys and sincere, toothy gals. At church camp the boys got to do the neat capers like chopping wood and building fires and digging holes. At church camp the girls had to do all the girl chores like set the table, cook, wash up. For activities after Bible class, the boys got to hike and fish and learn to use a compass in case they ever got lost in the woods. Girls got to do beadwork and decoupage and make pot holders. At church camp we slept in cabins, six or eight kids and one counselor to make sure we didn't tell ghost stories, which were against the Lord, or sneak out to visit the boys, which was temptation.

At Girl Scout camp, though, there were no boys so girls got to do all the chores including the cool, possibly dangerous ones. We got to hike and sail and ride horseback. You got to stay up late in your bunk which, whether it was in a huge, four-bedder platform tent or a Conestoga wagon replica or a cabin, was counselor-free, though they were comfortably within shouting distance in case you got afraid. You could scare each other to death with stories about ghosts or people who'd escaped from insane asylums or maniacs, or read with your flashlight under the covers or lay awake in your bed and think of your handsome counselor.

The counselors were usually college girls home for the summer. They were sporty girls in their late teens or early twenties who didn't wear makeup or ridiculous clothes and who liked the out-of-doors and living away from their families in a single-sex environment. They were girls who wanted to prolong their tomboy adolescence as long as they possibly could.

I'd been in Girl Scouts forever: Brownies in primary school, then Juniors, then in junior high, Cadettes, and finally, embarrassingly in high school, Seniors. Though only for a year because only the homeliest, nerdiest girls stayed in after that. I stayed in that long because of camp.

I liked the hiking and horseback riding and sleeping under stars. I liked being away from home and wearing shorts and a T-shirt and a sailor cap and swimming in a river or lake or pool every day and cooking beans and hot dog stew above an open fire. But also, I realize in retrospect, I liked the women.

Most of the counselors were sweet, long-haired girls who liked leading campfire songs and doing crafts and working with little kids. They were reliable young women who would go on to teach grade school or work in the helping professions or have babies of their own. At camp we didn't know them by their real names, but by "camp names." These names were to make them distinct from us, with our Beckys and Kathys and Dees, and suggest their friendly authority over us, while not sounding as formal or school-like as Miss Spencer or Mrs. Williams or Miss Pike. Counselors' camp names were meant to be fun or friendly or site-specific. They were usually names like Bandana or Dandi, as in dandelion, or Cricket.

But there were always a few counselors whose names were different. These were the counselors who were not so sweet, who occasionally smelled of cigarettes and did not go ga-ga over the cute little Brownies and would never, as far as anyone could imagine, have babies of their own. They were tanned, surly women whose hair was always short and who would never, ever, ever wear a dress. They did not have fun camp names like Cricket. They had no-nonsense names like Gunwale or Lanyard or Cracker or Dock. They were tight-lipped, wrinkled women and they were not just regular unit counselors, but special staff. They were the heads of sailing and riding and swimming, women more comfortable in the boathouse or stable or pool, with their equipment, the hardware of their work, than with children. They wore flexy watches and the sleeves of their T-shirts rolled. They were women without families, for whom Girl Scout camp was just a way to kill time in the summer, women whose real lives were lived as gym teachers or juvenile detention officers or in the Reserves.

There was a pair of them at riding camp, Davy and Lou. They were the only ones I'd ever known of with names like that, names that could be human, male, not cartoon names like Dusty or Spinner or Spoon. None of us ever tried to guess their names, the way we did with the other counselors, to see if they were Cindy or Marion or Rachel. We knew that their names were always their names; they were always Davy and Lou.

Both of them were quiet and tough, though Davy was quieter and tougher. They each had brown hair, Lou's curly, Davy's straight, but each so short you could barely see it coming out of the back of the wide-brimmed cowboy hats they always wore. They never cut up or rode like ruffians. They always rode sternly and quietly, as serious as John Wayne: back ramrod straight, one hand cupped loosely around the reins, the other resting calmly on the thigh. They didn't sleep in a cabin or tent like everyone else, but shared the trailer they drove to camp every year from wherever it was they lived. I didn't know where they came from but I wondered.

I wondered a lot about Davy and Lou. I wondered about their lives outside of camp. I couldn't imagine them living in a neighborhood like mine. The apartment where I lived with my mom was full of other overtired, working single moms and their millions of screaming kids and occasional boyfriends. I couldn't imagine Davy and Lou living there, or them with regular jobs like teachers or nurses or secretaries. I couldn't imagine them politely saying "yessir" to their bosses. I couldn't imagine how Davy and Lou would live in a world with men.

Their competence with horses, their terseness with girls, their difference from anyone I'd ever met before, the way they looked both frightened and excited me. I felt confused. I wanted and I did not want them to notice me. I wanted and I did not want to know about wherever it was they came from. I knew I wasn't like the sweet, long-haired counselors who were going to have kids of their own, but I also knew I could never be as tough and brave and different as Davy and Lou.

The last year I went to summer camp I felt old. Most other kids my age had become too cool to be in Scouts or go to camp. But a few other girls from my troop and I went. We were decent, hardworking kids who knew that going to camp was a way of getting out of our summer jobs—working for our moms or dads, or babysitting or a paper route—for a couple of weeks. We knew to take advantage of being young as long as we could.

These other girls and I had been friends for years. We had talked to each other about everything—our parents' fights and losses of jobs, our pregnant cousins and horrible younger siblings. We talked about our complexions and our weight and our crushes on guys. We talked about play try-outs and what we thought about God and all the things we were going to do when we finally got out of the boring Texas town where we lived. We tried to act ironic and we swore to each other that we would never, after we got to high school, refer to the fact that we had been to summer camp the previous summer.

The camp was divided into units, each with about twenty campers and two or three staff. The staff who slept in your unit were your regular counselors who you did most things with, like hikes and meals and capers and flag. But each unit also housed a special counselor or two from the pool or dock or kitchen or office. There were four units: Pioneer for

Brownies; Tanglewood for Juniors; Lakewood for Cadettes; and Brazos, for more Cadettes and the very few Seniors who still went to camp. My friends and I were in a cabin together in Brazos.

The cabins in Brazos were further apart than the tents or cabins in the younger kids' units so you didn't hear absolutely everything going on in the cabin next door. The front of every cabin in Brazos unit had a covered porch with a bench.

At the end of every day there was an all-camp campfire and all the campers and unit counselors were there. Sometimes the special staff came too. The only ones who were never there were Davy and Lou.

At most all-camp events you had to sit with your unit and your unit staff, but at the nightly campfire you could sit anywhere. We all sat around the campfire to do skits or stories or folklore or stars and, finally, right before we went to bed, songs. I think this was partly to make the little ones sleepy, the way lullabies do, but it didn't me. The songs were songs the Girl Scouts had sung forever. Some, like the ones by Joan Baez and Bob Dylan and other folk singers, were fine by me and my sophisticated cabin-mates, but others we considered extremely stupid. Some of the good songs were "Dona," "Blowin' in the Wind," "Michael Row the Boat Ashore," and "Kumbaya." The dumb songs were like "The Girl Scout Round," "The Smile Song" ("I have something in my pocket, it belongs across my face . . ."), and "Today." "Today" we considered the absolute sappiest. It was so sappy that our cabin began to cut up with it. We started singing it very loudly, extremely overdramatically. We pretended to cry, then wail. We put our arms around each other and swayed back and forth like we were being saved at a revival (which in fact I had been a few summers previous, but I was getting over it).

After the campfire we all filed back to our units and got ready for bed. At Lights Out you were supposed to go to sleep, but my friends and I considered it a point of honor to stay up at least a little late to gossip or giggle or whisper dirty jokes to one another. After my cabin-mates got to sleep, I snuck out of bed and went out on the porch. I liked how cool and quiet it was. I sat on the porch and looked out at the night and thought about things or I turned on my pocket flashlight and read a book.

One night, a few days into the session, I was sitting on the porch and I saw a flashlight on the path in the woods coming back to the unit. I thought if I went back inside whoever it was would hear me so I decided to just stay there and hope she didn't see me in the dark. I was up way after I should have been in bed.

The flashlight bobbed closer and I could hear this person walking. When she reached the clearing of the unit, I saw it was Scuff, the swimming counselor. She wasn't like the one the summer before who yelled at you when you couldn't do something then told you afterward it was to "make you work." When kids were scared Scuff talked to them, not down to them or in baby talk, the way some of the gushy, cheer-leader-type counselors did, but quietly. She also listened. And though her hair was as short as theirs, she wasn't terse like Davy and Lou. She hung around by herself or with everybody equally. Sometimes she made jokes that no one else got and she'd just shrug and smile to herself. I could tell she was smart.

When Scuff got out of the trees, she turned off her flashlight and looked up at the sky. There was a terrific moon. When she started walking again, I saw her see me.

"Hey," she called out to me quietly. "Hey," I called back. She walked over to the porch and said, "Mind if I pull up a chair?" I said, "Go ahead," and she sat down next to me.

She told me she was coming back from the pool. She'd gone swimming. You weren't supposed to swim alone. You also weren't supposed to swim at night. She didn't ask me what I was doing up after Lights Out or tell me to get to bed. She said, "So what are you up to?" and I said, "Nothing." I was sitting there with my book. She asked me what I was reading. I don't remember what it was but I had just started reading my brother's science fiction books, people like Ray Bradbury and Ursula LeGuin and James Tiptree Jr. She asked what kind of books I liked and I told her. She didn't talk to me like a counselor to a camper or an adult to a kid, but like one person to another.

I remember her profile, the line of her face that caught the line of the moon. I remember the movement of her mouth and hands.

After a while we stopped talking and it was cool and quiet and we listened to the night. It sounded close but also far away.

Then after a while she said it was getting late and she'd better get some sleep. She stood up to leave and I said I'd better get some too. I didn't watch her leave. I stepped back into the cabin where my friends were sleeping. These girls had been my friends for years, good friends I'd done a million things with, from study hall and book reports to first cigarettes and beer. But this time, for the first time, I felt apart from them. I felt different suddenly, like I had a secret, although I did not know what the secret was.

I crawled into bed. I lay on my back and looked up at the ceiling I couldn't see. I looked at the window and out at the dark. I didn't sleep.

The next day I didn't know how to act. I didn't know if I should pretend I didn't know Scuff had been swimming and that she knew I'd been up after Lights Out. I kept thinking of everything she'd said to me. I said her name to myself over and over in my head. I felt like everyone could read my mind and that they knew I was thinking of her. Part of me wanted to tell everyone, but also I didn't want to tell, I wanted them just to know without my telling, because I wouldn't tell because I was so cool about it. But I also wanted no one to know. I was afraid I'd get in trouble about being up after Lights Out but I was also afraid of something else I didn't know. I felt excited and confused.

I tried to tell myself it wasn't a big deal. Maybe she was just being nice, which was her job after all. Maybe she would talk to anyone she ran into, not just me. Maybe she thought nothing of talking to me.

I was eager and nervous to see her at swimming. The assistant swimming counselor was getting us into our lesson groups and everyone was running around. Scuff was at the deep end but she walked down to us and stopped me and said, "Hey, nice talk last night." "Yeah," I shrugged like it was no big deal. But I was thrilled.

I tried to swim my best that day but I swam terribly.

The rest of the day dragged by. I wanted it to be night, after Lights Out.

At campfire that night I couldn't keep myself from look-ing to see if Scuff was going to be there or not. I tried to be subtle but after a while my friend I was sitting next to said, "What are you looking for?" and I shook my head as if to say, "nothing."

The last song of the night was "Today" and my friends and I cut up again. We put our arms around each other's shoulders and swayed together that sappy way. Some of the other girls laughed but a couple of fussy counselors shook their heads. I was feeling superior with my friends until I saw Scuff at the edge of the campfire. Then, suddenly, I felt stu-pid, like my friends and I were so juvenile. I wanted to quit but I couldn't stop swaying between them. I hoped Scuff wouldn't see me but she did. She must have thought we were funny too because she was looking at us and smiling.

That night after Lights Out and after my cabin-mates were asleep, I got my book and my pocket flashlight and went out onto the porch and tried to read. I looked at the words and turned the pages but didn't take in much.

It wasn't that late when I saw her light, but it seemed like I had waited for it my whole entire life. I saw the white beam bobbing on the trees. I watched until she got to the clearing then I looked down at my book. I kept my pocket flashlight on my book and listened to her walk but I didn't look up. I only looked up when she said, "Hey." She was standing a few feet in front of me. "Hey," I said back. Then I said, "You wanna pull up a chair?" She laughed and said "Sure," and sat down next to me on the bench and we turned out the lights and talked.

She said we'd been funny when we were cutting up about "Today." I felt relieved that she didn't think we were being stupid. Then she asked me about the music I liked. My brother was in a band at college and my sister was a hippie and I had listened to their records for years so I had something to tell her that I thought was okay.

We were quiet for a while then she asked me, out of nowhere, if I could be anyone in history who would I be. I was still recovering from my recent bout of Christian fundamentalism and said, half-heartedly, "C. S. Lewis?" When she asked me why I said him, I shrugged. "I wouldn't really want to be him, I just can't think of anyone."

"I know who I'd like to be," she said. She paused then she said, "Gertrude Stein."

She asked me if I'd heard of her and I said I hadn't. She told me she was a writer, the one who said, "A rose is a rose is a rose," and that she had all these amazing writer and painter friends and a salon where all of them came. She never married but lived this incredible life with her roommate, another woman, in Paris. Scuff told me to be sure to remember her name.

After this we met on the porch every night and talked about all kinds of things, about books and politics and ideas. I believe she saw me as I was, a smart-enough kid who could get along alright, but also a different-enough kid who would, if not immediately, then sometime in the future, be grateful for what she gave me.

She didn't tell me everything. She didn't tell too much. She didn't want to frighten me, but tell enough to let me know that there were other, different, though still mysterious ways that I could live.

She told me that after the summer was over she was moving up north to live in a self-supporting community of women.

The last night of camp was the big all-camp campfire. Everyone showed up for the campfire, including the special staff and kitchen folks, even Davy and Lou. They gave out the patches to whoever had completed their junior lifesaving course or basic or advanced sailing or canoeing. Davy and Lou gave ribbons to the winners of the gymkhana. All the units got to present a skit or song and some of the counselors did too. The campfire went on very late, and because of that, but more because it was the last, and they, like all of us, were watching dying embers and falling stars and singing quiet songs, a lot of the little girls—some of the same ones who had wept miserably their first few, very homesick days of the session—who didn't want the two weeks to end, cried. They clutched one another's hands and sobbed on one another's shirts. My friends and I did not, of course. We were above all that. When the sad songs started, we snickered and sang off-key. At "Today" we draped our arms around one another and wailed. By then, some of the other girls in our unit had begun to ham it up along with my cabin-mates and me.

When we started on the second verse, Scuff left where she was standing with the waterfront staff and walked over to us. She reached her left hand out to me. When I took it she pulled me up, and as everyone started singing the third verse, while she kept my left hand in her own, she put my right hand on her shoulder and began to waltz. I knew some of how to dance from gym, where every year since fifth grade we had one day a week of square dance. I knew one person was supposed to lead—it was supposed to be the guy—and one person followed, who was supposed to be the girl. Scuff pulled me beside her carefully until I got her rhythm, then she dipped me, then hoisted me over her. When she lowered me we galloped like horses until she pressed the side of her face to mine, I could feel her body beside me, and thrust our arms in front of us for a tango. She slid her sneakers along the ground like it was a polished ballroom floor. Outside the circle of her warm, milky breath and my uneven gasps, I heard the whole camp sing and laugh and my cabin-mates whoop and clap. We did a square-dance do-si-do, then linked our elbows and spun. She took my hands in both of hers and twirled me around. I got dizzy. When I started to fall she caught me and held me up. I laughed and panted and caught my breath. I was glad the song was coming to an end. She held my shoulders to steady me. When the song was over, everyone clapped and shouted "Encore! Encore!" I knew I couldn't dance any more and hoped she could read that in my eyes, my tentative body. She shook my hand and bowed the way you do at the end of a dance. My head still spun, so I only nodded a little. She kept her warm, stable arm around me as she walked me back to my friends. She sat me down and before she left she squeezed the tops of my shoulders with her hands.

I was so tired and something else that I didn't wait on the porch that night.

The next morning after breakfast we packed our gear, the stuff we had brought and the stuff we had made and collected at summer camp, and waited for our parents or whoever to come pick us up. There weren't lessons that day, so I couldn't count on seeing Scuff at the pool. I packed quickly, then wandered around the unit to look for her, but she found me first. I heard someone behind me say, "Wild party last night," and turned around and it was her.

"Yeah," I laughed but then I didn't know what else to say. I stuck out a piece of paper and said, "Can I have your address?"

"Sure," she said. I was glad she didn't hesitate. "You got a pencil?" I pulled one from my pocket and handed it to her. She tore the paper and handed half to me. "Can I have yours too?" she said. She wrote her address while I waited. When she handed me the pencil, I wrote my name and address, and we gave each other our scraps of paper.

She'd written her real name, not her camp name. It was Nancy Booth. I couldn't bring myself to call her that out loud, but I hoped someday I might.

She tapped the address and said, "That's my parents', but it'll be good for a while. And they should forward stuff after I move."

I tapped mine and said, "That's my parents' too, well, my mom's, but I'll probably be living there a while." I said it like a joke because we both knew I was just starting high school and would be living at my mom's for years. It was a stupid joke, but she laughed.

I wrote her long, confused, and very earnest letters and she wrote back. Her letters were smart and funny and generous and also, I realized later, very careful to not lead me on. Of course she knew I had a crush on her, a colossal one, but she did not make fun of or take advantage of that. She could have.

In her letters she talked about ideas and books and, after her address changed, about the community of women she lived with in Chicago. They were writers and artists and musicians and they grew a lot of their own food and did their own plumbing and house repairs and mostly supported themselves as a printing collective. Some of the things she said about them reminded me of Gertrude Stein and her friends.

That fall, when I went to high school for the first time, I tried to check out a book of Gertrude Stein's from the library, but there weren't any so I went to the downtown public library and found some there. I kept going back there for more about Stein and then for other books I learned about from her.

We wrote for years, through several changes of address for her, through my entire high school career. Sometimes I wouldn't hear from her for ages, then I'd get a long letter about a trip she'd taken to Berkeley or Colorado or New Mexico. Sometimes she'd say she was moving and would send me her new address when she had it.

I don't remember which was the last letter I got from her, because I had no idea it would be, but after a while her letters stopped. I tried more than once to get in touch with her via her parents' address. Though those letters were never returned to me, neither were they answered.

Sometimes, still, I think of her. I think of her kindness, what she gave me, her example, and I wish I could get back in touch with her. I wish I could know what had happened to her. I want to know that her life is good. I also want to tell her that a tomboy she met years ago, a girl, like any girl, with her own set of pains and fears and mysteries was helped by her. I want to tell her I survived and I am happy now. I want to tell her I am grateful.

Nancy Booth, wherever you are, thank you.

A Vision

When I was six my family moved to Spain. My father was in the military and though my mother had not been happy with the peripatetic life our family led, she was excited about this posting. This posting would let her go to Europe and take her daughters, my older sister and me, to museums and historic homes and castles. My brother wasn't interested in any of that. Like my father, he preferred fishing. But "the girls," as my father and brother called Mom and us, loved going to museums. My sister, who wanted to be an artist, liked looking at the paintings. I liked looking at the armor. I loved those huge tall statues of silver and bronze, with their shiny shins and pointy, sectioned feet that looked like armadillos. I liked the plush royal blue and purple brocade and quilted cloth and chain mail. I liked looking at the face guards with slits and wondering what it looked like inside. I loved the plumes on helmets, the gold carved handles of swords. I loved the red-and-white striped and blue-and-gold checked skirts the statues of the horses wore. l loved the stories I was learning about the olden days. I decided that I wanted to be a knight.

My best friend was our neighbor, Chuckie Thom. Chuckie and I would get ratty old bath towels from our mothers and draw insignias on them with magic markers— dragons or castles or lions or gargoyles—and safety-pin them around our necks so they'd hang down our backs like capes. Then we'd run around waving our rulers or our big brothers' baseball bats as if they were swords and yell, "But my Lord, I am not worthy! I am not worthy!" while we stabbed out the innards and chopped off the heads of our imaginary foes. We'd turn garbage-can lids into shields and our fathers' pool cues into lances and joust or go on a mission to find my brother's baseball trophy, the Holy Grail.

Most often Chuck was King Arthur, but he also got to be Edward the Black Prince, Henry the Fifth, or Richard the Lion-Hearted. He had a choice. I, because I was a girl, was always Joan of Arc. Except for how she was burned at the stake and her religion, which I didn't understand, I liked Joan of Arc, so mostly I liked being her.

Sometimes, when Chuck had been called home for dinner and I played late alone, I would imagine things. I would get very, very quiet, then I would lift my arms straight up toward the sky, close my eyes, and tip my head so far back I would get dizzy. Then I would wait. I waited until I could almost feel against my skin, or at least in the air above my skin, a touch. Or if not exactly a touch, at least the passing of something through the air beside me, a spirit or someone right next, or at least, near to me. I waited until, although, because my eyes were closed I couldn't see, I could, almost, or so it seemed, see something like a figure, like a ghost, a shape, or colors, inside my tight-shut eyes. I waited until I almost heard, not in my ears, but in my head, a sound like someone saying something, whispering, as if someone was telling me a secret. I stayed like that, my head tipped back, my eyes shut tight and waited for, like Joan of Arc, a vision.

When we moved back to the states it was to Texas, where we had never lived before. The next year I entered sixth grade. All of the teachers at Stephen F. Austin Elementary School, home of the Fighting Rams, except the football coach who was also the principal, were women. All of the women teachers, except one, dressed up for school. Mrs. Kreidler, my homeroom teacher, never wore the same dress twice and her shoes always matched her dress. Once she brought a record to class and sang to us in her high thin voice, a song about the mountains. The dress she wore that day had a pattern of mountains and stars. Miss Bryant, the art and music teacher, wore pink or other pastels, usually suits with big shoulders and you could smell her perfume all the way inside the room where she walked in the hall. Mrs. Grant, the science teacher, was old and wore lots of powder and had bright, red, perfectly round circles on her cheeks and lots of shiny rings on her knobby hands. Sometimes she tripped on her heels.

Miss Hopkins, however, was different. She had short, straight black hair that she never curled and you could see that it was shaved at the back of her neck. She always wore penny loafers or flats, never heels. Her clothes were plain, black or gray or navy A-line skirts with light blue or white or beige open-collared shirts. She never wore dresses and never patterns or pastels. Her glasses did not have cats'-eye frames or pointy frames or frames held on with a gold-looking chain the way the other teachers did. Her frames were plain and black. She taught us math.

The first day of class Miss Hopkins told us that our grades would be based "strictly on class average," of all our homework and tests. Miss Hopkins did not give extra credit. There was no arguing, no Mickey-Mousing with Miss Hopkins. Everyone was afraid of her. Nobody misbehaved with her. Not even the football players or the cheerleaders.

This was different from other classes. Football was a huge, huge deal in our small Texas town. Football boys were let out of class to practice. Some of the teachers flirted with them, or with their dads, or looked the other way when the football boys copied from the smart kids during tests. Some teachers had been known to hold some big boys back a grade so they would be even bigger and play even harder the next year. Miss Hopkins, however, did none of that. She treated the football boys and cheerleader girls like anybody else. She treated everyone the same. She had no pets.

Every fall there were cheerleader tryouts and for the weeks before the tryouts our gym periods were devoted to learning cheers. We'd have class on the playfield outside where, instead of doing softball or track or even exercises, we did cheers.

I hated cheers. I was bad at them and couldn't get my hand claps and my jumps and arm flaps to coordinate. I couldn't do the splits and I hated the leg kicks that you were supposed to do in a line like the can-can. I hated the way you were supposed to wiggle your butt and smile and squeal and yell that high stupid way. But it was class so I had to do it.

Most of the girls, the Brendas and RaeAnns and Darleens, the cute ones, liked working on cheers and were looking forward to the tryouts. These were the girls who had a chance. But there were also the other girls. Girls with names like Carmen or Maria or Rosa, girls with the wrong religion because they were Catholic. Or girls who were fat or smelly, or wore dirty, old-fashioned clothes. Girls who only lived there for a while before they had to move again. There was one girl with a limp and one girl who had peed at a Girl Scout meeting once and one retarded girl. These were the girls who did not have a chance.

I didn't have a chance either, but not because I was Mexican-American or poor or fat. I didn't have a chance, because I didn't want to. I didn't want to be a cheerleader. I didn't want to wear the little skirts they did and worry—or hope—that the boys would see my underpants when I jumped up. I didn't want to go out with boys and I didn't want to act the way girls did when they were around them. I was the only girl in my sixth-grade class who did not try out for cheerleader.

By the time I went to college, in 1975, very far away from Texas, I wrote poetry, listened to cool music, ate vegetarian, had sex with boys and girls my own age, and told stories. It was fun to tell my artsy, liberal, drunken, feminist young friends stories about Texas. I shaped the story of my not trying out for cheerleader as a mock heroic tale of escape from an oppressive, southern-style femininity. Though I was a white girl who got to go to college, I allied myself, in my retelling, with the Mexican girls and fat, poor girls who couldn't get away the way I did. I attributed to myself a sassy rebelliousness that I had never actually had as a kid. In fact I was self-conscious and any rebelling I ever did I only did in private.

A lot of my life occurred in private, more and more of it as I slipped away from childhood and toward whatever difficult thing was coming next. More and more I imagined things. I often did not understand them or admit them to myself and I certainly never told them to anyone else. But I imagined some things so earnestly, so hopefully and longingly, that in my mind, I think, I almost saw them.

It's right after tryouts and it's a huge, huge deal that I have not tried out. It is the talk of the school. It is notorious. I go to Miss Hopkins.

No.

No—She comes to me.

She comes to me. She puts one of her handsome hands, for I have looked at her hands and they are handsome, square and firm and very, very clean with short, round nails. Her watch is facedown on her wrist, not faceup like the other women's watches and the band is dark brown leather, not thin and gold-looking like a bracelet. She puts her handsome, competent hand on my shoulder. I feel it on me. It feels firm as if it steadies me, but also light, like pulling me, like lifting me toward—toward—

I can smell her skin, like Irish Spring soap, right next to me. I feel so much, like everything. And I can hear, I think, the sound of the air, its breath, as if the air is alive, around her marvelous, marvelous hands.

She leans her face down close to me and says, her breath like mint, "I heard you didn't try out for cheerleader."

I cannot say—I don't—but I don't need to, no, not anything—

Because she knows.

I look at her and, for the first time ever, see behind her glasses. Her eyes are blue, lighter than blue eyes usually are, like ice, but also with a warmth to them, like water you could fall into and it would sweep you away. I see her start to smile, her thin lips somehow fuller, softening, and the skin creasing around her mouth and I see the shine on her white, white teeth, one canine slightly sharper than the rest. Her tongue is wet. I hear her do this little laugh, then something else from inside her throat as she removes, first, her plain black-framed glasses, then mine.

She tips my head back a bit and I close my eyes and tip my head further back and I am very still then feel something near my skin and hear a whisper, telling me—

I can't hear what she says.

Of course that didn't happen.

Not that, exactly. Not exactly then.

Her name was not Miss Hopkins. I was not thirteen.

But someone sometime somethinged me. There was some thing I almost felt, if not beside my body, then above me, in the air. Something or someone passed nearby. Or someone came toward me and I heard, almost, if not a voice, then something, then I saw and someone kissed me.

Though neither that, exactly.

I kissed *her.*

★ ★ ★

It happened later.

She turned around a corner in the hall I couldn't see. (Though I have seen it since, yes, many times in memory and still I do.) She stepped down the steps by the window in the hall I was standing in. I was talking to someone else who I forgot immediately because already it had happened.

I saw, in the light of the late afternoon, the perfect light go over her. I saw illuminated her perfect face, her slightly open mouth. A brilliant light surrounded her. It pulsed around her everywhere and I was almost blinded. Her hair was black, her eyes were blue, her mouth was slightly open. There was a way she breathed, the way her chest and shoulders rose and fell. There was the way her throat moved when she swallowed. There was the line of the throat. There was the cup in the flesh at the base of her throat. There was the light in the air around her. She was beautiful.

I wanted to put my mouth on her. I wanted to eat her alive. I wanted to possess her, to devour, to consume her. I wanted to . . . something . . . her into next year and back and back again. I wanted to, with her, annihilate myself.

I was, however, half her age.

For this and other reasons this did not occur.

Not then.

Later.

Later I went back to her and took us to the bed. Therein did we do what we were meant.

I still believe, despite the rest, that this was good.

I loved her.

I saw in her the possible. I saw the real embodiment of what, in some way, I had longed for years. I saw she whom, though I could not possess, I might hold for a time.

I believe what I remember.

I believe that what I saw and did continues in a place outside of time, that it remains.

I believe that what remains occurs and will again.

I believe the vision I was shown, the body I was given.

I believe what I desired was made manifest as love.

This is what I tell of my religion.

The Smokers

All of us used to smoke cigarettes. My brother smoked Winstons. I don't remember what my sister did because she became hippie and got into health food and natural everything including pot so she quit. My mother smoked Salems and my father smoked filterless Camels. I was the youngest, so I started last and by the time I was really smoking there were low-tar and nicotine brands like Merit and Vantage and I smoked those. In any event, I never smoked as much as everybody else did. Smoking was not my problem.

After my father left, my mother switched to Benson and Hedges. Then after he'd been gone for a while, she used a graduated filter system that was supposed to help you taper off until you quit. She went through all the steps, the first filter that took out a little, then the next one that took out more, then the next one that took out even more until the last one they said let through almost nothing, as if you practically weren't even smoking, but my mother couldn't get past it. She kept smoking with that last filter for years.

I remember her cleaning out the filters, twisting a Kleenex

into a point and sticking it in and the Kleenex coming out covered with sticky brown sludge. She'd do three or four until there was not much sludge on them then she'd put the filter back on another cigarette and light up.

She was good about cleaning up but sometimes one of the Kleenexes would fall on the floor and I'd find it, dust and hair and lint sticking to it, and I'd pick it up and throw it away and my hands would get sludge on them. The dirty Kleenexes were also in her car, on the dashboard and the floor and in the crack of the seat. They were also all over the bottom of her purse.

There were ashtrays all over wherever we lived—in the military units and apartment buildings, in other peoples' homes while they were away, in a hotel one time, in all of the rentals my mother said someday she'd like to buy.

There were ashtrays all over everywhere. On the counter by the sink in the bathroom. On the end tables in the TV room and on the coffee table in the living room. On the bar in the kitchen. On the picnic table out on the back porch. The outdoor ones were those heavy, tinfoil-feeling ones, round, but with a corrugated edge so you could put a lot of butts in all at once. The outdoor ones were left outside so after it rained they were filled with scummy, tea-brown water that had floating in it ashes, filters, filth. There were ashtrays on the worktable in the garage where my father oiled his guns, on the ledge by the hose out back where he cleaned his birds and gutted his fish and skinned his rabbits. There were ashtrays on the tables on either side of the bed in my parents' bedroom and then, after my mother moved into the spare room, which had been my sister's before she'd gone away to college, on the orange crate on the side of that bed, too.

There were ashtrays in their cars—her big, fake wood–sided Ford station wagon in which she shopped and hauled us kids around; his tidy, compact, perfectly white Peugeot. The ashtray in the Ford was crammed, broken, lipstick-stained filters poking up out of it and falling on the floor and rolling around with the crumpled hamburger wrappers and french-fry bags and the waxy Coke cups and straws from whatever our mother had grabbed for us when we were late and she didn't have time to cook. The door to that ashtray would never close. It was always, no matter how often you emptied it, crammed. On the floor of her car were those tough, skinny, gold-colored strings you opened the cellophane with and empty wrappers, some almost whole, the top part opening up like a lid or flopping back and forth like a broken neck. There were parts of them, curly pieces, irregular triangles and little strips, slivery pieces that clung to your skin and ragged pieces she had torn open with her teeth.

The ashtray in his car was never crammed. It was always, like the rest of his car, well tended, neat, and to the degree he could control it, childfree.

My mother's ashtrays were ceramic, home-thrown pottery, avocado or aztec gold or burnt sienna, the colors women were using in the art classes she was always going to take. Though one of them, in a nod to the hippies, was chartreuse.

My father's ashtrays were fat, thick, heavy ones from the military, clear glass, square, each corner pressed in with a pencil-thick dent where you put the cigarette. My father also had round ashtrays, brass or copper looking, but in fact some kind of yellow stained aluminum bowl on a bean-bag base. There was a metal strip across the top of the bowl with three little dents for cigarettes. These ashtrays were on the dinner table and by the magazine rack in the bathroom. The military ones, which he preferred, were on the table beside his big chair and by his stool at the kitchen bar. The butts in my father's ashtrays were short, smashed squarely, almost tidy. He smoked them all the way down to the end then put them out with one firm press. My father did not like to be interrupted at a smoke. He preferred to smoke deliberately, with a drink.

My mother never smoked them all the way. She smoked them nervously, between stirring something on the stove or answering the phone or changing the laundry. She never carried a cigarette from one room to the next. She said when a woman walked with a cigarette it made her look cheap. My mother smoked when she was trying to sit down for a minute between things. There'd be a cold cup of coffee from when she'd tried to sit down before but then remembered a phone call she had to return or heard the buzzer go off in the laundry or a pot boil over and in one frantic movement she stood up, sucked in a drag, stubbed it out, often breaking it because it was still so long, and ran to the phone or laundry or kitchen.

Her ashtrays were full of broken sticks, the paper jagged at the break, shreds of tobacco poking out of them like splinters. Her ashtrays were full of long curled straws of ashes, like fallen-down columns. My father said to her, more than once, that one of these days she was going to burn down the goddamned house.

There is a photo of my parents at a luau. It looks like it's from the early sixties so I must have been around by then, but

I do not remember ever seeing them like this. My mother is wearing a shoulderless shift. Her neck and upper arms are firm and fit. I can see the delicate bones of her collarbone, her neck. I can see the line her skin makes when it goes from her ear to her neck. I know the skin of her shoulders is smooth.

She's sitting at a low table with six or eight other adults who all look about her age. The men, all white, wear Hawaiian shirts. Some of the women, not her, have flowers in their hair. Her hair is dark and wavy and long. I've only ever seen it like that in pictures. On the table is a watermelon or something stuffed with—I can't see exactly—banana? melon? canned pineapple? There's a platter of things on skewers, bowls of rice and, though some people are drinking from coconut shells, others have regular highball glasses. My mother is talking to the woman next to her and holding a cigarette. This picture, of course, is still, but I can tell my mother is not gesturing with her cigarette. She would not do anything to draw undue attention to herself, would never cheapen herself like that. She holds the cigarette like a prop to make her look confident and sure, as if she belongs, and also as if she has a wonderful secret. My father stands behind her smoking too, a Camel in his right hand. He's talking to a fat guy laughing at something someone has said. My father is smiling at the man, but I know his smile is not because of something anybody's said, but because his other hand, the one without the cigarette, is resting on the smooth and naked shoulder of his pretty, sexy wife.

My sister was the first of us kids to start. She was in high school. My mother caught her.

My mother and I had gone out somewhere—I don't remember where—and come back early. My sister had snuck into the bathroom, stuffed a towel in the crack at the bottom of the door, and tried to smoke. My mother could smell it the second she walked in the house. She went straight to the bathroom and tried the door—it was locked—and called my sister's name. My sister didn't say anything. Then there was a frantic sound of flushing, some rumbling in the trash, and my mother rattled the door and shouted, "I know what you're doing in there, Betty!" I didn't know how my mother knew it was my sister and not—he was only one year younger—my brother.

"I know exactly what you're doing in there!" my mother shouted again.

She sounded angry but also, in some way, triumphant, like this was one thing about which she would not be fooled.

There was also something sad in her voice. She was seeing her elder daughter alone and curious, afraid of being caught but needing to investigate this adult, forbidden thing. She was seeing her daughter turn into her.

When my brother started growing his hair long my father hated it. They fought about his hair the way they fought about the war, about the career in the military my brother didn't want to have, about his music and what he ate, about him no longer wanting to fish or hunt; they fought about everything.

Then one night when my mother and sister were spending the night over in Dallas to look at a college my sister had applied to, the fighting between my father and brother got physical. I was in my room, where I spent most of my time, reading a book or listening to a record and I heard them yelling in the living room. I turned the record up and stared at the door and hoped it wouldn't open.

I heard my father's angry voice, then nothing, then my brother mumbling, then my father again, louder, then my brother, louder too, then yelling—I couldn't tell which—then it was both of them, then something crashed, then something else, then there was a scuffling sound then something falling, then pushing, then a sound like breath being caught, then running, an opening door, a slam, more running, then they were outside and I shut off the record and my light and pulled the curtain aside the tiniest bit so I could see outside without being seen. My brother was running down the street, away from my father but also turning back to yell and curse at him and call him terrible things. It sounded also, though, like he was crying. My father jogged raggedly, wheezing, across the yard to the curb where he stopped and panted and watched my brother run. I saw my father from the side, his chest and shoulders heaving. I could hear him breathing very hard. He watched until we couldn't hear my brother any more. Then my father pulled his hankie from his pocket and wiped his face and neck. I heard him gulping air. After his breath began to calm, he made a sound like an old, defeated animal.

The light was out in my room. I was hoping my father would think, if he noticed at all, that I was asleep. It was not that my father would bother me: he never did. It was that I didn't want my father or brother or anyone, including me, to have seen what had happened between them.

The last thing I remember was my father, after his son had left, sitting wearily down on the roadside curb where he slipped a Camel from his shirt and lit it up.

My mother would not smoke around her mother. We went to visit my grandmother in Oklahoma City almost every summer. After my brother and sister had grown, I took this trip with my mother alone. My grandmother knew her daughter smoked, and that her son-in-law, of whom she had never approved, did so as well. She also knew he drank.

My mother's mother despised smoking. She thought it was a filthy, cheap thing for a woman to do. A few times my mother and I went out to the grocery or a movie or museum without her mother, but most of the time we were at home with her. There were no men—my grandfather was dead, my father was gone, my brother was away at college—so we stayed at home and did the things that women did—cooked and cleaned and worried and remembered.

After her mother went to bed was when my mother would smoke. She only smoked outside and only on the back porch, not the front where someone might see her. As if to compensate for what she'd been denied during the day, she smoked several, all the way down to the filter, one right after the other, then smashed the butts into the jar she had in her purse for this, then dumped them into the trash behind the garage.

Sometimes I'd go out onto the porch with her. I wouldn't smoke—I was still young—but I would sit with my mother and talk. After the hot, dry day, the air was finally cool and my mother no longer had to behave the way she did around her mother.

"You looking forward to starting school again?"

"Yeah," I said. "I guess." I missed my schoolfriends over the summer. A lot of people went away.

"Kathy will be home when we get back, won't she?"

"Yeah." Kathy, my best friend, was one of eight kids in a big Catholic family. I spent a lot of time over there. Sometimes we babysat the smaller kids and sometimes we just hung out and listened to records. Kathy liked Dan Fogelberg and Simon and Garfunkel. I liked the Beatles and the Kinks and the Who but we got along anyway. Every summer Kathy's parents took all their kids to visit their Uncle Chuck in Colorado. He had a lake.

"Did you decide about Spanish or French?"

"I think Spanish," I said. Most of the smart girls took French, like Spanish was just for the Mexican kids, but I liked it better. Also, Senora Schwartz, the Spanish teacher, was nicer than Madamoiselle DuVall who Kathy and I and our friends thought was, as we loved to say, "soooooo pretentious." My mother thought so too. I had introduced my mother to Madamoiselle DuVall one time when we ran into her at Safeway and afterward in the car we'd both laughed like crazy at her accent. Everyone knew Madamoiselle DuVall was from Plano, but she always tried to do this stupid accent when she met people.

My mother was working as a Welcome Wagon Lady but she didn't like to talk about her job: What she liked to talk about was school. She was going back to college at night to become a social worker. Sometimes we did our homework together, her on one side of the table and me on the other, each of us surrounded by our books. Sometimes she told me about what she was reading in her political history and sociology and anthropology classes and we talked about what I was doing in English. Some of these times she seemed happy, like something good was just around the corner.

But out on her mother's porch, when she was smoking in the evening, my mother sounded tired. I tried to cheer her up sometimes, but I hardly ever could.

After my mother's father died, the front curtain in her parents' house were always drawn. The house was dark and so quiet you could hear a clock ticking in the next room. My mother was in her early forties then, which seemed very old to me. I knew my mother didn't like being at her mother's house so I didn't understand why she kept going there. I didn't understand how long you stay your parent's child.

My mother smoked her first cigarette on the train to Sophie Newcombe Women's College in New Orleans. She'd wanted to go there, very far away, to study speech and drama. It was the farthest she'd ever been from Oklahoma, the longest she'd ever been away from her parents. The train took a couple days. She went by herself. It was the biggest adventure she'd ever had, then even bigger when the train broke down in the middle of the night and everyone woke up and people roamed the corridors in their robes and pajamas talking. At first everyone seemed concerned and scared but then they opened the café and it became, my mother told me, like a party. They were way out in the country, nobody knew exactly where. It was dark outside, but mild and warm and people stepped on and off the train in their pajamas and robes, with their drinks, to walk around in the damp, still air and look at the stars. When somebody asked her where she was from and where she was going and to tell him all about herself, and offered her a cigarette, she took it.

I smoked my first cigarette during the year I spent abroad on a high school scholarship. In England, where I lived, I smoked Silk Cuts and Players. In France, where I visited, I smoked Gitanes and Gaulois. In Spain, where I also visited, I smoked something really cheap called Escudos and coughed and hacked all night. I bought a pack of cigarettes every other day there and smoked them instead of eating breakfast or lunch. I only ate one meal a day, dinner, late at night, which I thought was very Continental. Once, with a girl who was the granddaughter of a man who made millions importing them, I smoked these incredibly potent but very smooth Russian cigarettes, Sobranies, that were wrapped in elegant black paper.

During that year I also got drunk for the first time and had my first sexual affair. When I came back to the States I told my mother about the smoking but not about the drinking, which she still hated about my father, nor about the sex.

The first year I lived away from home was also the first year my mother ever lived alone. She had lived with her parents for seventeen years then in a dorm at Sophie Newcombe for a year (until she transferred to Oklahoma where she met my father), then, after she got married, with my father. After my siblings were born and my father was away on tour, she lived with her children. After my father left for good and my brother and sister were away to college, she lived with me.

When I came back from my year abroad, I lived my summer before college at home with her. She said if I was going to smoke anyway, she'd rather I didn't do it behind her back and started bringing home with her, when she got in from work, all different kinds of cigarettes for us to smoke together.

We tried the new ones—"You've come a long way baby" Virginia Slims and the long, skinny "silly millimeter longer" 101's. We tried Benson and Hedges menthols, which were my mother's usual brand and Benson and Hedges regular. They had the best ads. We tried the old ones, like Newport, which were only smoked by blacks in the ads, Kools, and my mother's former brand, Salem. Menthols had green packages—forest green or kelly green or icey mint green. The regular ones were usually in red packages with white or black or gold trim. I wanted to try Lark because that's what Ringo was smoking in a picture I remembered of the Beatles. Plus they had that great jingle, "Have a lark, have a lark, have a lark today!" to the tune of the William Tell Overture but they tasted horrible. We also tried Winston, Marlboro, Old Gold, Parliament, Lucky Strike, and Kent. My mother didn't like any of the regular ones. She said if it wasn't a menthol she might as well not even smoke at all.

The only brand we didn't try was Camel, my father's brand.

Every morning when he woke up, my father coughed wet, thick hacks. I'd hear him in the bathroom clearing his throat like he was saying "a-hem," "a-hem," "a-hem," over and over, hawking. When he came out of the bathroom he would get a cup of coffee my mother had perked and sit down with his newspaper to do the crossword. After his cup of coffee, he went back to the bathroom to cough and hack some more then on his way back to the table he would grab a bottle of Dos XXs from the fridge, pop it open on the bottle opener at the end of the kitchen bar, and sit down with it. My mother would come over to warm up his coffee but he would not acknowledge her. He'd take a swig of his Mexican beer and another drag of his cigarette and get back to his crossword.

One of the few times I remember my father playing with me when I was little was this game about counting the letter "e's" on the back of his pack of Camels. He'd ask me to count them and I would try to but I always missed one or counted one too many times and I never could remember from one time to the next how many "e's" there were. I remember the package, the camel, the pyramid in the background, the skinny lines of sky, the gold and yellow and brown that made it look like Egypt. I remember how far away it looked, how exotic, dark, and masculine. But I could never remember how many "e's."

I do remember the crinkle of the cellophane when my father opened a new pack, that gold string around the top with the little opening where you were supposed to pull it. I remember my father tearing the cellophane all the way off and crumpling it into a little ball and throwing it into the trash. It sounded like a mouse or a tiny animal that slowly, as if secretly, although we all already knew that it could not, was trying to escape.

My father told me about "three on a match." During the war, by which he meant World War II, cigarettes were one of the men's only rewards or comforts. A cigarette could calm a soldier down or maybe, for an instant, be the only thing that might get a man's mind off his pain. My father told me how some guys would light a cigarette for a wounded man, one in pain, "real pain," my father would say, because this wounded guy couldn't light it for himself. You'd have to light it for him and maybe even put it in his mouth and he'd just barely be able to suck on it, it would just barely hang there, quivering, on his bottom lip and he'd drop ashes on his chest but not even notice, even if it burned, because he was already in such immense, incredible pain, "real pain."

My father told me this with his face half turned away from me, as if the mere remembering was painful to him. He wanted me to see that I would never—no one who had not been in the war would ever—understand the pain of being in the war.

Three on a match was bad luck because you could light one buddy, but never two buddies because by the time the third cigarette was lit the Germans would have spotted you and you'd be shot.

My father didn't say these things like they were common stories anyone who'd ever seen a movie knew. He told me them as if they had happened to him.

I didn't know, when he was telling me these things, that my father had never fought in the war. I learned this from my mother after he left. Then, when both my parents were dead, I learned from my father's brother that my father, from the time he was very young, had wanted to be a soldier. Their father had been in the First World War and when he came home he brought his gun and taught my father and his little brother Stan, who were six and three, to clean and care for it. As soon as my father was old enough, he enlisted. He was accepted into pilot training school, but by the time he finished training, the Second World War was over. Though he made a career in the navy, my father never saw an active day of combat in his life.

I believe my father saw this as his shame.

After my father died, I went to see his widow and pay my respects. (She was his third wife; his second had died of food poisoning in Mexico.) My father's third wife started telling me what a shame it was that my father had destroyed his medals.

"What medals?" I asked.

"The medals he got in the war," she said. She told me about his heroism and how he'd been rewarded but then how, crushed by the country's response to Vietnam and his long-haired, hippie, teenaged son's refusal to volunteer, he had destroyed his medals.

"I see," I said. "That's too bad." I had never heard of any medals. I almost asked her why my father had never shown these medals to anyone else—like his first wife, my mother, who welcomed him home from the East, or his son who had once played soldier like other little boys, but I realized this would just be cruel. I had nothing against my father's wife. She'd always been kind to me. But there was something in me that wanted to show my father up, that wanted to hurt him by exposing him as a fraud to someone he had loved.

One summer I was going to go visit my father and his third wife and he told me Little Brother, which is what he called my Uncle Stanley who was his favorite person in the world, was going to be there too, with my cousin. I was glad. It was easier to disappear if there were more people around. But I also really liked my cousin and she liked me. We were the same age, the youngest in our families, and kept going on trips with either of our parents after our siblings stopped. I also liked Uncle Stanley. He was our cool relative. He had moved to Canada, which was cool, to take a job in the oil business up there, but his passion was music. He played trumpet in a jazz band and didn't hate the Beatles the way my father did, but actually thought they had some, as he said, "great little tunes." He would listen to our music and smile and bob his head and say, "Beautiful! Beautiful!" the way my father only ever talked about airplanes.

When my cousin was telling me about her parents getting divorced, which they did a few years after mine, she said it was like whatever his big brother did, her father had to do, too. My cousin and I considered each other allies.

The last time we had seen each other, also down in Texas where we'd all come to visit my father, we were in junior high. Now that each of us was in our first year of college, our fathers had decided to treat us like adults. Partly this was a compliment and partly it was awful.

My cousin and uncle got there a few days before I did. The day after I got there we all drove down to Mexico. This was a trip my father and his wife did a few times a year. They tried to coordinate it when the dollar was strong, go down for a couple of days and stay in some hotel—"It doesn't have to be fancy," my father would say, "but it does have to be clean. And have some decent goddamned service." During the day my father's wife shopped and he sat by the pool and read Mickey Spillane novels and drank and in the late afternoon they went out for drinks at their favorite bars then stayed out for dinner at their favorite restaurants then had after-dinner drinks somewhere else. After a few days of that they'd drive home with their full allowance of booze.

We got in the car after my father woke up and drove for hours. There were five of us—the two men in front and the three "girls" in back. It was hot outside, that dry, stingy summer Texas heat, which is even worse on the highway so we had the air conditioner on and the windows all closed. My father smoked the whole way down. He must have smoked a pack. The smoke in the car got terrible. My cousin and I, squashed together, kept looking at each other and rolling our eyes and making puke faces and mouthing "I TH-INK I AM GO-IN-G TO RE-GUR-GI-TATE," but neither of us dared to say anything. Our fathers were talking up front completely oblivious to whatever was going on in the backseat and my father's wife, practically as soon as she got in the car, had made this big, huge yawn and announced in her chipper voice that she was "just beat!" and closed her eyes and went to sleep. My eyes were watering, my cousin's too, and after a while we closed them and pretended to sleep. We kept them closed the rest of the trip.

When we got there, even before we checked into the hotel, we went to this restaurant and had a couple of sloe gin fizzes each and then a couple of bottles of wine with lunch and by the end of lunch I was tipsy enough to ask my father for a cigarette. His weren't menthols like my mother's, but regular. They were also unfiltered. My father looked at me a couple seconds, then chuckled, then tapped one into my waiting hand and lit it for me gallantly.

At the hotel my father said he needed a nap and we all agreed to meet later for dinner. As soon as we got to our room my cousin and I fell onto our beds and burst out laughing. "Jesus Christ," I said, staring up at the watery ceiling, "Two o'clock in the after-fucking-noon and we're already completely smashed!"

"God," she said, "I can't remember ever having so much to drink."

"Jesus," I said, "Fucking—A. . . ." I didn't want to close my eyes.

She groaned then asked, "Do you think this whole trip is going to be like this?"

"Yep," I said.

"Oh god," she groaned again. I sat up and saw her holding her head. My head was aching too, and my throat felt rough but I knew that wouldn't stop me from drinking and smoking more later. I went to the bathroom to splash water on my face and drink a couple of glasses. When I came out to the room I was going to tell my cousin we could buy some strong Mexican aspirin when the shops opened up again but she was asleep.

The next days were pretty much the same, except I bought my own cigarettes so I wouldn't have to keep bumming them off my father. I got filtered but not menthol: regular.

My mother stopped smoking a few years after she moved away from the last place she lived with my father. My mother moved to a small apartment by herself and then, after she retired, to a small town and bought a house. It was the first piece of property she had ever owned. She had a garden and a cat and she was happy.

My father stopped smoking when his doctor told him that his third wife, who was not a smoker, was inhaling the equivalent of a pack a day by being around him and therefore more prone to cancer. My father quit cold turkey.

Throughout their ten-plus years of marriage, my father called his third wife "my bride." I believe my father had finally found the kind of love he'd always wanted.

But then, shortly after he gave up smoking, my father had a stroke. His doctor said his body might be reacting to the sudden deprivation, after daily doses, for more than fifty years, of nicotine.

Though my father survived, after the stroke his memory slipped and his speech slurred. These things weren't new, but the stroke allowed us to talk openly about them because we could pretend the stroke had caused them.

I remember the bathroom gray with steam from the shower and smoke from the cigarettes. I remember the burned spots on the linoleum floor, the burned holes in the carpet. I remember the once-white, yellowed curtains, the smoke-stained walls. I remember the yellow scum on the paper towels when I Windexed the windows. I remember emptying ashtrays in every room, the matches, the wrappers, the butts. I remember the smell of them in the trash, the butts and stale ashes. I remember the ashes around the sink, in the dishwater and the toilet. I remember them flicked and spilt and thrown on the floor. I remember the smoke that slowly rose into the stale, yellow air.

My mother died first. The death certificate called it an "expected" death. We had discovered her colon cancer when I'd gone down to see her the previous summer. I was able to quit my job and go care for her during her last six months. My sister was there a lot too and my brother came down when he could. Chris, my partner, was able to be there sometimes too, including the night my mother died.

Then six weeks after my mother, my father died. His death was not expected. Although for decades we had wondered how anyone could live the way he did, there was no "precipitating event" that made his death seem imminent. His wife told us he'd said he felt like taking a nap and headed down the hall to their room but an hour later, when she saw the light on in the bathroom and knocked and there was no answer, she opened the door and found him on the floor and he was dead.

Between them my parents had three kinds of cancer — colon, skin, and prostate — as well as high blood pressure, bad circulation, anemia, shortness of breath, and heart and respiratory failure. I have no doubt their smoking contributed to, if it didn't actually cause, these conditions.

But I also think, for years their smoking saved them.

Within a few years of when they were married, the exact date of which I have never known because they never, at least in my or my siblings' memories, ever acknowledged much less celebrated an anniversary, my parents were deeply unhappy with one another. Smoking allowed them to take a break and get away for a while from whatever was making them miserable. Smoking was something they could each look forward to. They, each alone, could get away from us kids, the noise, the crap, for a quiet smoke. Or they could, each alone, drive to the grocery store for a new pack when the cartons my mother had bought at the Navy PX had run out, then make their way back home as slowly as they could. Smoking was a pleasure that, though they had once enjoyed together, they grew to prefer alone. He could do something for only himself and imagine he was strong and tough, a hero of the war. She could do something for only herself and imagine she was above it all, unfazed and cool, like a woman in the movies. They each could imagine other lives. They could each imagine their shitty lives weren't shitty.

I'm grateful for this. I'm grateful they had something to help them get through their terrible years. I'm grateful they got to live long enough to quit and then to finally, for however brief a time, live happily until they had to die.

An Element

My father was a navy man. As long as he worked, he worked on water. He was a pilot on an aircraft carrier. He loved flying. The only thing above him was sky, below him water. He loved sighting the carrier then tipping, swooping, aiming down, and landing perfectly on deck, the way the water underneath him moved. He loved the life of a man at sea— the whup of the wind and the suck of the wave and the voices of men without women. He loved spending months away from land and being out of touch with anyone not a sailor.

When he went ashore, he liked to go to exotic places— Singapore, the Philippines, Japan. When he had to come back to his family, he spent as much time as he could out on the water with other misplaced servicemen home on leave.

My father went out early, before any of us kids were up. The nights before he went, after I had gone to bed, I'd hear him getting ready for his trip. He'd stack his rods and reels by the door, his tackle box and the big black net with the silver aluminum handle he used to pull them up with. He'd get out his many-pocketed vest and his cap. Sometimes he'd take his waders and an extra change of clothes. There was a smelly package of bait in the fridge, and sometimes worms, which my mother hated. My father would put his thermos out on the kitchen table. It was a big, green, no-nonsense thermos, not a light, little, colored plastic thing like I took in my lunchbox to school. My mother would wake up with him and make him a breakfast he wouldn't eat, and sandwiches for the road. She would fill his thermos with coffee.

For a while, before he could buy his own boat, he went out with other men. My brother and I begged our father to go along but as long as he was a guest in someone else's boat, he said, he couldn't take us.

As soon as he could afford it, my father got a boat of his own. It was bigger than the car and had a huge Evinrude outboard motor. He moved the boat in the garage and put the car out into the street. We wanted him to take us out in it but he wouldn't. "The boat is not a toy," he said. "It's not a place for kids." The boat was also not a place for women: "It's bad luck to have a female on board," my father said. Though at first my mother balked at this, she didn't complain for long. We all knew she was afraid of water. My sister didn't ask to go out on it. The only thing she would have liked about it was the boys. But my brother and I would sneak into the garage and climb around in it. We'd peek inside the neat little drawers and cabinets that lifted up beneath the seats. We'd look at the neatly knotted ropes, their different widths and colors, at the anchor and chain and the see-through plastic boxes and Styrofoam cup holders and bean-bag-bottomed ashtrays, at the compass and the steering wheel which we would always try to turn but it was locked.

* * *

My mother feared that she would die by water. A drowning or a tidal wave, a flood. For years she feared that she and her family, by whom she meant her children, would be destroyed by it. But she also, very cautiously, loved it.

She kept her head above the water when she swam. Because, she told me, she had "broken her eardrums" when she was a girl. This sounded ancient to me, like polio or rickets or diptheria. It made my mother's childhood seem very long ago.

She swam the dog paddle, her head above the water, her arms pulling out in front and to her sides. There was no way to do it gracefully. She wore a bathing cap, her hair tucked up beneath the pink or green after-dinner mint or aqua-colored rubber. Some of the bathing caps were plain, with the slightly knobbled texture of a basketball, but some of them had patterned grooves to make them look like waves or leaves or flowers. Some other womens'—not hers, she'd never wear something so showy or cheap—had big soft, squishy rubber flowers or anemones stuck on them. The women who wore them wore bikinis or skimpy two-pieces, which were often too small for them and their bosoms fell out of the sides and they looked like whores. My mother wore a modest, tasteful one-piece.

My mother did not like putting on the caps. I could see it in her face, as she stretched them out and pulled them down on her head, I could see in her eyes when her hair would catch and her skin would pinch. She'd tuck her hair in but it wouldn't stay. The caps smelled like rubber, chlorine, stale.

I suppose it was inevitable, that these two people, such different people, after they had gotten over their initial attraction to their opposite, would hurt and be hurt by each other. For years I hated the way they were with one another and I blamed my father. I saw my mother, who continued to raise us after our father left, as the good one. But now that both of them are dead, and I no longer fantasize that my father will have some great revelation or change of heart, I am becoming able to forgive him. I am beginning to see my father as a misplaced man who didn't know how to live outside of his element.

One summer we got a cabin by a lake. We pulled my father's boat behind the car. When our last car had died, my mother wanted to get a station wagon with room for her and the kids, but my father wanted a car that could pull a boat. He got his way but only after he promised my mother he'd take the kids out in the boat.

Lake Texarkana was a day's drive away but my father had heard it was great for fishing. The last few miles to the "resort," which turned out to be a bunch of dumpy little cabins, was unpaved and full of ruts so we were dusty and dry-mouthed and even more cranky than usual by the time we got there. But when we finally got out of the car, the air felt cool and fresh. My mother sighed and my brother jumped up and down and whooped and my father didn't stop him. I found a place where I could look through the trees to the lake. The lake looked black. I couldn't tell if I was seeing into it or only the reflection of the sky.

My father and brother went down to the dock to put the boat in while my mother and I settled into the cabin. Because my sister was a high school senior who everyone knew would be completely miserable spending a week at a lake with her family, she was staying in town with friends. This was the first time I was the only one helping my mother do something like this and I wanted to do it right. We put the clothes and towels and luggage in the rooms and I went out and picked flowers and set the table and helped my mother put the food away in the kitchen.

One way our mother had convinced us to agree to take a "family trip" was to allow everyone to bring along some of the bad food we weren't allowed to eat at home. So we had regular food, like milk and cheese and lettuce and bread and hamburger meat and canned corn, but we also had vacation food like Charles's potato chips, which they delivered to our house in big beige cans, the thick ruffly ones my brother liked and the barbecue flavored ones my sister liked and I pretended I liked too, and huge bags of cookies and licorice and after-dinner butter mints and cans of Hi-C. My mother and I put the good food in the cabinets and the bad food on the counters along with my father's mixers and drinks.

The cabin had two bedrooms and a bathroom and a main room which was also the kitchen. My brother and I were supposed to share a room but he wanted to sleep on the couch in the main room, which was fine by me.

There was a window in my room and I remember lying on my cot with just a single sheet over me at dusk when I went to bed and hearing lots of different birdcalls and imagining canaries and pigeons and eagles and doves settling down in their branches and nests and the tops of trees. Then later, when it was dark outside and I heard twigs snap and leaves crackling, I knew it must be deer and raccoons and bears. I tried to guess which by how heavy or light their feet sounded on the twigs. Then later, when it was getting cold and I had to pull a blanket on, there were other, different, far-off sounds, that I couldn't exactly tell if I was actually hearing or not, but I thought I was. I heard, or I imagined I heard, in the deep black, still black water, fish and eels and anemones and waving, swishing plants, but then also things not moving, still. Or moving so very, very slowly you couldn't see them move. Or even things that were not actual things, but something else down in the deep and watery black.

The next day he took me into it.

Before he let us in the boat, my father reminded my brother and me of the rules of the boat: The life vest is to be worn at all times. Shoes are to be worn at all times. And by shoes I mean *shoes,* not goddamn flip-flops. Rubber-soled shoes only. Getting into and out of the boat will be done carefully, slowly, to maintain the balance of the boat, which must always be maintained. Never jump onto or off of a boat. Never jump on a boat, period. More boating accidents occur near the dock, due to the monkeying around of people who did not know or respect boats, than out on open water. The boat is not a toy. The boat is a vessel and your father is the captain of the vessel.

Our father had told us these things many times before when the boat was up on the trailer at home but he told us them again. He had also, because our mother had said he had to take us out, tried to teach us some of the knots. My brother could do some of them but the only one I could do was the square knot that we had already learned in Girl Scouts. My brother said it was the easiest one.

So when my father finally took me out with him and my brother on Lake Texarkana we had already been taught about how to behave on a boat. The person my father hadn't taught was my mother.

My father showed my brother how fast it could go. When we stopped riding around and having fun, my father cut the engine and dropped the anchor and he and my brother caught a lot of fish. I had a rod and reel too but after a while I gave up and just sat there. They got very excited when something snagged one of their lines. When they saw the bobber bob, they would jump up—my father didn't reprimand my brother about jumping then—and one of them would reel it in and the other one would grab the net and put it underneath the fish when they brought it in. I tried to help for a while, but then I just tried to stay out of the way. I sat on the bow and looked down at the water. I closed my eyes and I could feel, even though we were still, the water moving below us.

It was late when we got back.

As soon as we could see that my mother was waiting for us on the dock, my father slowed the motor down. He didn't want her to be able to say he'd been being reckless. My mother was sitting on a chair she'd brought down from the cabin. I didn't know how long she'd been sitting there, but as we got closer, I saw she had a book. My brother and I started waving to her. My brother jumped and started to shout about how

many fish he'd caught but my father told him to quit monkeying around and pay attention because we were about to dock.

My father slowed the motor, but kept it going. He turned
the wheel so the boat would go into the dock sideways, like
parallel parking. I heard the motor purring and I could smell
the gasoline. I was up on the bow. My father told me to
loosen a rope and throw it to my mother so she could tie us
up. I threw my mother the rope, but it didn't go far enough
so my brother scrambled up beside me, dragged the rope back
to us and tossed it to her. That time she caught it. By then
the rope was wet and hard to hold. When my mother tried
to pull us in, the rope kept slipping from her hands so she
wrapped it around her forearm. My father who, in addition
to steering, was also packing up the fishing stuff to unload,
didn't see her do this. Then she yanked the rope.

The boat turned suddenly sideways and my mother
stumbled, as if the rope was going to pull her into the water.
My mother screamed. My father looked up and saw her
stumbling toward the edge of the dock in her flip-flops, about
to fall in.

Goddammit! he yelled as he grabbed the wheel, goddammit, you idiot!!

He may have turned the wheel too fast or knocked the
motor up a speed or both. But whatever happened, the rope
around my mother's forearm tightened and yanked her
down. She fell. She screamed and her body was being
dragged along the dock.

My brother tried frantically to untie the rope from the
boat but he couldn't. My father shut the motor off entirely
and grabbed a paddle and started paddling toward the dock.

The boat knocked up against the dock and my brother and I almost fell. I jumped on the dock to go to my mother. I could feel the boat tip beneath me when I jumped. I helped my mother unwrap the rope from her arm. She was crying and sobbing, she couldn't think. Her arm was bleeding. My brother jumped off the boat and tied the bow rope to the dock then he hurried around to catch the rope from the stern my father would throw him.

When my brother had tied up the bow and stern, my father started handing him things from the boat. My father started to say things to my brother. His voice was very calm and he was talking about the way things should be packed onto the boat and the way they should be brought off the boat and how the privilege of being on the boat comes with responsibilities and how everyone who enjoys the boat needs to accept these responsibilities and do their part. My mother and I were already walking back up the dock. She was still crying. Her face was wet and her arm was bleeding and I was thinking of how to take care of it: Wash it with soap and warm water, then put on lotion where the skin was red and Band-Aids where it was cut. But when my mother heard him talking to my brother like that, she took a deep breath and wiped her eyes and turned around and walked back down the dock. I followed her. We carried the things he told us to, the things he couldn't carry alone, back to the cabin.

When I was a child I loved the water. I was also afraid of it. The first memory I have of it was when I almost drowned. I must have been four or five, not old enough to be on my own, but old enough to want to be. We were at a beach, the very first time for me. Before I'd always lived inland—in Kansas, Oklahoma. My mother, whose family had once been farmers, felt safe, almost happy in these places. While my father, whose mother had run off to New York City to become an actress when he was a boy, was always itching to get out of them. When he was home my father was restless to get back to the sea. I think my parents thought his getting stationed in Florida would help.

My brother and sister were out in the water swimming and yelling and splashing each other. I could see my brother jumping up and down, and making wide sweeps of the water with his arm and splashing my sister. My sister squealed as if she hated it, but you could tell she really liked it. She splashed him back, both hands pushing at him, like a girl. She dove in and he followed her. I saw her legs, then his, kick up. They looked wet and shiny, happy.

I was sitting on the sand alone. I was supposed to be playing. I was near enough so my parents could see me, but far enough so I wouldn't hear what they were talking about.

I wasn't on a towel, just the sand, and it was sticky and scratchy and hot.

Maybe my father went back to the car for a drink or maybe my mother went back for some lotion. Maybe the one who was left to watch me fell asleep or got caught up in their book—her Agatha Christie, his Mickey Spillane—or maybe they just, for a moment, forgot.

I remember going out into it, the wet and cool against my legs, the sand that slipped away. I remember seeing my brother and sister shimmering out in front of me. They didn't seem far. They didn't see me trying to reach them; no one did.

The water is cold, but not uncomfortable, oddly exciting. Sand squeezes up between my toes and water slips over my bony feet, then slaps against my ankles, slipping up my calves. It sucks against my knees and climbs my thighs. It tickles like a climbing bug then suddenly, when it reaches my panties, it is ice. The cold spreads up my belly and my bathing suit looks like something's spilled, then there's a splash, a gulp, and then the water's pulling back, the waves are going out. My skin is stippled cold. I stand still in the same place, but the water goes in and out. I feel it soaking in my suit. I sweep its shiny surface with my palms. My hands feel cool and slippery and I go further in.

Then suddenly it's at my chest and I am tumbled backward. It feels almost like falling, I am turning, rolling, looking up at the sky again, then there is water in my mouth and nose and I am spinning down. Then I am blinking, coughing, sputtering, then up again. I see the top of the water—foamy, creamy-looking—then my feet can't feel the ground at all— I am suspended—then roll again, I'm caught within the wet, its mouth and hands. It's folding me and turning me, I'm turning into it. Inside its mouth, I see the ends of plants and leaves and ropy things and swaying things, then something lifts me out—I gasp the air—then I am down again, unbreathing, blacking out—

I feel like I am something else, like something not connected to a thing. I am a plant, a leaf, a ropy thing, a skinless thing, the water.

Something sucks me further down. My head and chest are underneath. The water's dark. I kick and thrash and try to yell, I try to breathe—I'm sinking down.

I see the ends of my hair in front of me. The tips of my hair are swaying like plants. My hands are trying to push, to reach—

I do not know who rescued me. I do not know who brought me back.

Was it my father? Did he, despite the way he seemed, have a sense, some way he knew I was in danger? Or was it my mother? I remember her crying, her red, splotched face. Or was it someone else? A stranger? Someone passing by? Someone who heard my mother cry? Or did something, someone, push me up? Who made me come up out of it? Who pulled me out from where I was to air?

My father taught me how to swim.

It was in a motel pool. Whenever we traveled they tried to stay in some place with a pool so the kids would have something to do. My sister would sit by the water and put on suntan lotion. She'd wear her sunglasses and brush her curly hair as if that would make it straight, and try to get a tan but not get freckles. Her reddish hair was thin, like our mother's, and it frizzed out in high humidity and my sister always said, only halfway teasing, that she hated me because my hair didn't. My hair was blond and wavy like our father's. My sister sat by the pool in her sunglasses and looked at magazines that told you how to dress and how to diet and put on makeup and get a boy. My brother tried to hang out with her and be cool, but he always ended up jumping in the water and playing with the younger kids we'd always meet at these places. My sister would roll her eyes behind her sunglasses and shake her head and sigh very loudly at how immature we were.

My father sat me down by the edge of the pool then slid in the water beside me. I remember the springy hair on his chest and his freckled arms, the water beading off of him. The sound of him slipping in was quiet and smooth, like something that belonged in the water, an otter or a seal. The water was cold and there were prickles on my skin. My father eased me in the water there beside him. He turned his body so he was facing me and my back was to the side of the pool. I was holding onto the edge, my arms stretched up behind me. He took my hands in both of his and stepped back into the water. I felt my back pull away from the wall behind me; he was pulling me. He pulled my arms out taut, took one step back toward the center of the pool. The water rippled behind him. The sun made rings across it, light like jewels.

"You can do it," my father said, "Just try to reach me."

He pulled me from the solid side. I felt the water suck behind my skin. He squeezed my hands in his.

Then he dropped me.

I remember the drop of his hands from mine, my desperate lunge for his suddenly distant body. I remember his stepping away from me, his garbled voice as my head went under, "Try to reach me." I remember the stinging wet in my eyes. I remember the feeling of falling.

The water was heavy and everywhere, but nothing I could hold. I opened my eyes. His body stretched and waved like melting rubber. I kicked and opened my mouth to yell. I choked. I heard him call me from above. I yanked up my head and pawed. His hands were inches away from me. I stretched out but fell back again. I couldn't reach him.

Chlorine stung my eyes and throat. My heart beat in my

ears. Everything around me looked like waves, like light and dark, like something turning into something else. My father yelled above me, "Just reach out to me!" I sputtered, legs were jelly, hands too small. I couldn't hold the water.

"Come here," my father called, "I'm not that far." His hands were always out of touch. Each time I sank I rose more tired. I knew that I was drowning and I wouldn't reach my father.

Then, with the very last drop of strength I had, I stretched to where I thought he was and scraped against the rough edge of the concrete. I pulled my head up, panting. My father's huge hands grabbed me and he hoisted me out of the water.

As he plopped me down on the edge of the pool, he said, "See, honey, you swam that far."

He pointed to the other side, across the frantic water I'd stirred up.

"You came all the way across that by yourself."

I spat out water, gulped the thin good air.

My father put his solid arm around me, held me close.

But that was only for an instant.

Then awkwardly, squarely, he placed his hands on my shoulders, clutched them firmly as though they were bigger than they were and laughed, "You see that, babydoll, see what you can do? You crossed the whole thing by yourself."

He nodded at the wide expanse he'd lured me across.

I remember the oily wet of his chest, the solid even ticking of his watch, his hands I'd tried so hard, and failed, to reach, around my heaving shoulders.

I loved to dive down into it and stay deep down as long as I possibly could. I would imagine I was something else, a seal or an octopus or fish. I liked the cool slick way it felt, but also liked its heaviness, the way it covered me all over and how I had to push through it to move.

I'd swim far down until I could almost touch the drain, but then, my lungs about to burst, I had to kick back to the surface. I remember the first time I reached the drain. My hand stretched out in front of me and my fingertips scraped the concrete. Then I spun around and kicked against the bottom of the pool and shot back up. I loved the way my body gasped—the heaving chest, the beating blood. I knew I was alive.

My mother feared that she would die by water. A drowning or a tidal wave, a flood. She dreamed of these scenarios and woke up from them screaming. One hurricane season in Texas, a time my father was away, there was a flash flood. It was at night and she was driving me home from somewhere and she drove home through it. We were okay, and our house and car, but the next day in the paper we read about people who'd gotten stuck, whose living rooms were flooded or they'd lost their pets. We even read about a baby who went missing.

I loved to dive down into it and stay deep down as long as I possibly could. I would imagine I was something else until, about to burst, I had to kick back to the surface.

My mother didn't die of it, but of its opposite. She died because she couldn't keep enough water. She became dehydrated. Her bladder and kidneys shut down and she couldn't process water, but she still felt thirsty. She looked at us with glazed, yearning eyes. Her toothless mouth moved like a baby trying to suck. The nurses had given us these little sponges on the ends of these Q-tip type things that you could put in her mouth for her to suck on. The sponges had this minty stuff on them too, so they smelled good, which we were glad about because everything else smelled terrible, like medicine or death. Even if she could suck these things, she wouldn't get enough water to make her kidneys and bladder work, but only enough to moisten her mouth. We put them in her mouth and held them while she sucked. I remember the way the stick moved when she sucked, the feel of want. She was trying to suck but she couldn't swallow. When I pulled it from her mouth it had strings of saliva on it, white spots of things.

Later her eyes were vacant, like a fish's eye. Her last few days she didn't speak, she just made sounds, sometimes like a frightened child or a sleeper's moan, but sometimes not like anything else at all.

My father died ungracefully.

He was doing his crossword puzzle at his table in front of the TV. His wife was on the couch beside the table with a book. He told her he was going to take a nap. This wasn't unusual. He often took naps in the afternoon. He drank a lot with lunch. He got up from his crossword puzzle, his widow told me afterward, and started down the hall.

Their bedroom was at the end of the hall, past the bathroom. I remember when I had stayed with them years before, going into their room to get something one of them asked for, and seeing some of the furniture I'd grown up with—his father's dresser, his mother's marble-topped nightstand, his German beer mugs. My father's father had died when he was young, his mother when he was about the age that I am now. I remember not wanting to look at the room. I didn't want to look at their private things, but I noticed. The books they kept on their bedside tables—his Robert Ludlum; her Penelope Lively. Their scruffed and soft-looking slippers on the floor. Her hairbrush and his wallet and keys and dish of change on the top of the dresser. Their photos of her kids.

His wife told him to have a good nap. He waved goodnight to her and he headed down the hall.

Later she noticed a light beneath the bathroom door. She knocked and he didn't answer. She tried to open the door but it stuck. There was something up against it. She pushed the door. She had to push it hard. She had to lean her body into it. When it opened she saw him on the floor.

I think of him falling in that room. I see it over and over in my head like a movie loop. It happens slowly, again and again. I see the shiny white porcelain bath and toilet, the knobbled, damp-darkened throw rug, its coiled, matted threads, the roll of paper towels on the counter—they're white but with little blue and purple flower print—and the can of air freshener with its yellow "lemony" plastic push-button top. His toothbrush and his razor and his aftershave. Her brush and comb and makeup pads. The spots of toothpaste on the mirror.

But I don't know what actually happened. Did he clutch his chest and tumble? Did he fall against the toilet or the tub?

Or did he see himself, his startled, frightened face, white, in the mirror? What did he see?

Did something flash before his eyes? Did he cry out? Did he remember us?

Did he fall forward, knock his head against the counter or the tub? Or hit his head? Or did he crumple, knees and ankles buckling, hands thrust in front of him to stop him? Did he know that he was falling?

I picture his knobby knees—the ones I get from him— buckling, hitting the side of the tub, then him slipping to the floor. I see his head hit the side of the tub or the side of the toilet, his rose-white flesh, his freckled skin, hitting, then bouncing, then hitting again against the porcelain.

Did how he feel feel new? Like something he had never done? Or only done that once when he was born? Or did he feel a way he'd felt a lot before—like dropping fast through altitude, from cold high air down back to earth? Or did it feel like tipping backward off the boat, his nose pinched tight? Did it feel like diving into something deep?

Did he call out for his wife? Or someone else? His mother? Father?

I didn't see my father dead. He'd always told his wife he didn't want a funeral or service of any kind. He had already been cremated by the time I got to his widow's house two days later.

He'd also told his wife he wanted his ashes scattered over the ocean. He wanted them thrown from a naval aircraft carrier like the kind he'd served on when he was young. The local navy base was willing to do that, but they couldn't have civilians aboard. They wouldn't let his widow on the boat, so some navy men he'd never met were the ones who threw him over.

At first I thought this was awful: My father had remained so alienated from his families that his memorial was conducted by strangers. This was so different from my mother's death. Her children and siblings had all gathered around her so intimately during the last months and then the last moments of her life and were all able to say good-bye to her and love her. My father's sudden, isolated death on his bathroom floor felt tawdry. I didn't get to see or talk to him before he died and I felt cheated that we weren't able to acknowledge him in any kind of formal or ritual way.

But the further I get from my father's death, and the more detached I get from the impossible things I wanted from him, the more I can feel compassion for him. I can see now how right, how good it was that a group of navy men were the ones to scatter my father's ashes over the sea.

I think of those ashes floating down, the fine gray dust burned clean and pure.

Then I see his body whole again, healthy and fit and young. His hair is wavy and blond and his eyes are clear. He sparkles in his uniform, the bright gold band around his officer's hat, his polished buttons and shoes. His shirt is ironed crisp and he smells freshly shaved. There is a semi-circle of tall, uniformed men around him. My father salutes to them, and they salute back to him. Then my father spins on his shiny black uniform shoes and faces the end of the boat. He steps up onto the end of the boat, first one foot, then the other. When he's all the way up, he stands straight and tall for a second, then he takes his hat by its shiny black rim and flings it out over the water. Before his hat begins to fall, he dives off the back of the carrier. His body makes a smooth and elegant arc in the air, then it cuts into the water, barely breaking a wave. Then he is swimming, healthy, whole, embraced. My father pulls his arms back firmly and breathes deeply. But it is not air he's breathing now, not of this difficult world that broke him down, but somewhere else. I see his head, as smooth as a seal. He turns to look back one last time. I don't know if he's looking at me or saying good-bye. I do know he looks happy. Then he dives down deep, at last, where he belongs.

Breath

We sat in her house and listened to her breathe.

When we heard her breathe we knew she was still alive.

It had been several weeks since she had walked. It had been weeks since she had stood on her own, since she had eaten anything solid. It had been days since she had been able to drink or take her pills through her mouth. The water we gave her we gave on a sponge. We put it in her mouth and she closed her mouth around it and sucked. I couldn't tell if it was will or conscious or involuntary, the way a baby would suck. She didn't look at us. That is, sometimes her eyes would turn in what we thought was our direction, but we couldn't tell if she was seeing us or something else, something beyond or past us. We couldn't see if she was seeing anymore.

Her body sweat. The sweat would pour from her and we would change and change again the sheets around her. Sometimes her body was very hot, her skin would flush with what the nurses called the terminal fever. At other times her skin felt cold. That happens when, the nurses said, what regulates the body's temperature breaks down. There are upper brain functions and lower brain functions and you can see the body shutting down in order.

It had been a while since anyone had tried to put something in her porta-cath or tried to find a vein to give her something new. She was beyond what anyone could do.

The last thing that she did alive was breathe. For days and nights we sat in her room with her, or in the rooms where we tried to sleep, and listened. We listened as her breath got short and ragged, as she seemed to gasp or gurgle, seemed to hold her breath. The periods of this got long. You'd count up to ten or twenty and you would think she wouldn't breathe again but then she would. The nurses called this apnea. They said that it began before the end.

We listened and we waited. We listened after hope.

This was in the winter and we had the heat turned on. When the furnace clicked on it hummed and clanked and you couldn't hear. If you were watching TV or a video, you turned the volume up. Then when the temperature got where you'd set the thermostat, the furnace would click off and you could hear again.

My sister sat in our mother's room and listened to her breathe. The heat clicked on. It stayed on several minutes and then, when it clicked off, the room was quiet. My sister counted to ten, then twenty, then more. Then she came to the room where I slept and I went with her to our mother's room.

There was no more the sound of breath. There only was the sound of something gone.

My Mother s Body

A few days before my mother died, I said to my sister, I want to prepare the body with you.

We were in my mother's living room. Our mother was in her bedroom down the hall where she was dying. She was asleep or resting or whatever it was, on morphine or Haldol and other drugs the names of which I no longer remember. There were a lot of drugs but none of them were to help or cure anymore, they were only there for comfort.

She had taken drugs that might have helped. She had tried chemotherapy because she wanted to fight the cancer but it had terrible side effects. She got nauseous and exhausted. Her entire body ached. She bled from her mouth and vagina and nose. She lost her hair and her gums and lips became cracked and bloody. She couldn't eat from nausea and from the bleeding from her mouth. She couldn't shit then couldn't stop. The smell of cooking, of food, made her sick and she vomited. She vomited nothing, spit and air, because she couldn't eat and there was nothing to wretch up. She heaved and made these gurgling and hacking sounds as she vomited pills and spit. She vomited yellow phlegm and blood, thick strings of it, or clots, or clear and running.

The doctors had done everything that anybody could. They said she could quit taking chemo anytime but she didn't want to, she wanted to fight. We told ourselves that the side effects meant that the drugs were working, that the cancer cells were dying.

But then she became so weak and dehydrated that she had to go to the hospital for fluids. It was a week before she was due for her next round of chemo, which they decided to put off until she was stronger. So she didn't get chemo for several weeks but the side effects continued. Then the doctors said it wasn't the chemo causing those things anymore, it was the cancer. There was nothing else to do anymore except try to diminish the physical pain of her dying.

She lay in the bed in her room down the hall while my sister and I sat whispering in her living room. It was not her bed, but a hospital bed, brought in when she went on hospice. It had bars.

It was late at night and though our mother was asleep and couldn't hear us, we acted as if she could, as if we might wake her. We might have once. She was always a very light sleeper, especially around her children: She was vigilant. So my sister and I were acting the way we had been raised, to whisper when we were near someone sleeping.

We'd begun to whisper a lot in my mother's house. Before we knew how sick she was, when we talked with her docs on the phone, sometimes we'd whisper. "She picks at her food," we'd say. "Should I make her eat?" "The pain is still in her shoulder. Should I give her another pill?"

When our relatives called early on, we'd whisper little triumphs, "She ate four bites of mashed potatoes today!" "She only vomited twice!" Or, "We walked her out to her garden today."

Later when she was sick unto death, we'd whisper to them, "If you want to come see her, come soon."

The night my mother died, my sister came into the room where my partner Chris and I slept and said "Chris?" and I shot out of bed. I went to my mother's room and touched her, her face and her pulse and I saw her face and I said to my sister and Chris, "She's dead." Chris touched my mother and said she was. She was dead.

I don't remember what I did. Did I cry out loud or say something? Did I lean over my mother and kiss her? I don't remember. I remember my sister getting onto the bed and holding my mother and crying and saying, "Momma." When she got up, Chris lay beside my mother, too, and held her and thanked my mother out loud for loving her. I remember my sister, either with something she said or with a gesture, asking did I want to lie with my mother too and hold her goodbye but I couldn't.

Her face was yellow and waxy and smooth. Her cheeks were flat and her eyes were sunk and one of them was open. I tried to close it. Her head was shiny and almost bald, with just a little fuzz of hair where it had started to grow back when she stopped the chemo. It looked like a baby's, soft and white.

For days my sister, Betty, and I, and Chris after she arrived, had gathered things for my mother—rose petals from a bouquet from the boys, sage and basil and rosemary, for remembrance, from her garden. Betty'd brought some mugwort from an herbalist who told her it would bring clear dreams to the dead. We'd found an old green glass pitcher with a cork in the top and an old bronze vase of my grandfather's.

My mother's body was covered with sweat. We had been changing her sheets and the night shirt she was wearing several times a day, but she'd break into sweats as we changed them. Sweat would pour down her body. I didn't know how she could have so much when she hadn't been able to drink at all for days.

We washed my mother with warm, clean, sweet-smelling water. I remember the bowl with the water in it, and my sister and Chris and I each dipping our hands or cloth into the bowl, and washing my mother's skin. We took turns holding the bowl and took turns washing.

Her body was hairless as a girl and it was smaller. She'd lost so much weight and her skin was loose. But when we washed her, lifting her hand, her arm, her foot, her neck, she gave to us. The tension in her body, how it was stiff and clenched and could not bend or be turned easily the last days of her life, the twitching and the rigidness her body had had for days had been released.

The doctors and hospice workers had said she was past feeling, that the twitches and groans that came from her were only involuntary. They said her brain stem was functioning at the very lowest level, to make her lungs breathe and her blood circulate. They told us she was not aware and that her body could not feel anything.

But it was hard to see her twitch, and hear her throat and mouth make noises that sounded almost human, almost like speech, as if she was trying to tell or ask or beg us for something, for mercy perhaps.

We washed our mother's body and we talked to her. Her body was limp and gave to us. We washed her slowly and tenderly, as if she could still feel us, or feel us again. We washed her skin and told her that we loved her and we'd remember her. We thanked her for her life, for being good to us and kind. We told her that her body's pain was over. We told her we'd take care of things. She'd worried about things when she was alive, that she had left a burner on or hadn't locked a door. She worried about her children, if we had eaten enough or were warm or safe, if we felt cared about and loved. We told her everything was fine, that things were taken care of, she could rest.

Her skin looked flat and yellowish and felt, beneath my hands, like wax, still warm and soft and pliable.

We turned her over and changed the sheets then covered her with jasmine-scented oil. It was massage oil I had brought to her one time. My mother had never had a massage before she got sick and didn't really want one at first, but she got used to them. Every night whoever was with her, my sister or brother or me, would rub her shoulders and back and neck, her legs and arms and feet to help her sleep.

I poured the oil in my sister's hands, then Chris poured it into mine and hers and we covered my mother's body with oil. The room began to smell so clean. Our hands were soft and slippery. I remember the touch of my mother's skin, beneath my fingers and hands, the way she felt:

We poured red wine into a cup and drank. Then my sister put her hand in the cup and touched her fingers to our mother's mouth and spread the wine along her lips.

We covered her with flower petals and herbs that we had gathered from her garden. We tucked the charms her son and her grandson made into her open hands. We wrapped the clean white sheet and then her father's woollen blanket around her. We covered the flesh that had carried her, the body she had borne, that she had birthed us from, the body from which we had washed the final sweat.

When this was done we lay her down in her bed alone as if she could rest until morning.

The next morning we called the funeral parlor and a guy came out. He was young, a big, husky Mexican-American guy dressed in a nice suit and shiny black shoes. He smelled fresh and clean, like aftershave. We were wearing jeans and shirts. My sister's hair was still wet. We'd slept, probably the best we'd slept in ages, but there was something not quite awake about us. It wasn't until after the funeral guy left that I saw I was wearing my slippers.

The guy was gentle and soft-spoken and he let us take our time. He was very kind to us. My sister's face was red and puffy from crying. Chris was calm and I was very practical, like "We need to do this," "I think we ought to do this." Jo Marie, the hospice nurse, was there too. We'd called her earlier, about eight o'clock. I remember Chris and my sister and I discussing if we'd wake Jo Marie up, but she'd told us to call her anytime and had given us her home phone number. She was expecting it.

When the funeral guy got there the body was prepared so all we had to do was take her out.

You were supposed to put the body on this stretcher and wheel it out of the house. The funeral guy was looking at the hall and trying to figure out the best way to get the stretcher in and the body out and I said, "Can we carry her? I think we should carry her out." I tucked the sheet and blanket around my mother's face to cover her. My sister and Chris and me and my mom's next-door neighbor, her best friend, got on either side of the bed and put our hands underneath her to carry her. I could feel the wool of her father's blanket—he'd had it when he was a young man in the First World War—and we lifted her out of the bed.

She was cold by then. I could feel that through the blanket. She didn't feel like a person who was alive. She was stiff. This made her easier to carry in one way, though she was heavier than I expected.

We carried her out of the room and down the hall, through the living room and out of the house.

Outside, the day was beautiful. It was early Sunday morning.

We carried her to the driveway where the van was backed up. The guy opened the back of the van and we put her in on this cot thing. The guy strapped her to it and locked the wheels on the bottom. The wheels were so you could roll them out easily for where they'd burn.

When we put her in, the blanket slipped and you could see the top of her head. Her head was bald and looked pale and small. It looked like a baby's head, like a baby pushing out of its mother getting born. I went up and tucked the blanket back over the head as if to keep it from getting cold.

Description of a Struggle

I am trying to describe it again.

It has not changed although it slipped from me and then, because I needed to, as always I have done, I misremembered.

Although I can't forget entirely for always it remains.

Always it was here except for sometimes.

Although perhaps that's not the case.

It may not have been when I was young.

When I was young I was not as I am. It may have been but I nor knew nor recognized.

I was, when I was young, resilient, full of hope. I had not learned to not have hope.

I am no longer young.

Always it is here except for sometimes. Especially when I think that I'm about to stop, succumb, be fed to it, pressed underneath, for which I would not be ungrateful, no would, rather, please, I prithee—

It releases me.

I am released not by a thing I do but it.

Whatever is done is done by it. Whatever I do is naught. I nothing am.

Then it lifts me and I am again.

Then I am grateful then ashamed of being grateful, even glad to be at all again.

I'm grateful, when it lets me go, as if it has been kind to me.

I make these tearful promises. I say that I have learned this time, as if I have not learned before, as if those other times were naught, although they weren't, they were, they are, still, yes, each, every one of them, yes, all, I bear the marks, see, here, where I am bent, the lines and cuts, the bruises, scars, the nightmares, the prosthetic.

I pick myself up gingerly, the hand, the knees, the forehead, scraped and bloodied. Gravel in palm, dirt in cuts across the knees. The hair in clumps. Abrasions across, lacerations within the protrusions (forehead, nose, cheekbones, chin). The nails chewed and bloodied. The back swaybacked from the pushing down. The bones of the elbows chipped from attempting to hold up, though not succeeding, the belly not entirely dragging but almost. The shirt flapping, spotted with holes, the cloth apparently ancient though in fact recently young, care with the appearance having gone by the by some time ago, the collar frayed, the ends of the sleeves frayed, their color a ruddy rusty red, a sanguine hue, browning, blackening, expanding in spots, the rest of the shirt something of a shell-gray beige suggesting what once may have been white, clean, young, or new though no longer, however, is. The end of an arm is a stump.

The knees have been heroic. With the stump and the hand they too have attempted to remove themselves. The knees are hairless, scraped, bloodied, though not scabbed, having never been given sufficient respite from crawling to form into scabs. They, rather, have been in contact with the ground apparently constantly which is gravelly, gritty, grainy, sandy, with little splinters of glass therein, sticky, dusty, hot in spots, you could fry an egg on it some days, icy in others, lukewarm, as if you had spit it out of your mouth in others, slippery when wet, wet, severely slippery, as if covered with a thick layer of oil or grease, either auto, truck, or otherwise — black ice it is called in these parts, a dreaded road condition — slanted, sloped, cliffed, so either one is clawing oneself up against the pull of gravity against which one *cannot* argue, it has its laws, or one is clawing with what is left of one's nails or ersatz nails, gore or stitches, to keep from slipping sliding falling being dragged by the pull of gravity, against which one *cannot* argue, it has its laws, down. The knees, hand, and stump continue to be gushy, gunky, gory, gross, gelatinous in part, deeply unpleasant on the whole, yet also with stitches, unsightly undoubtedly, yet nonetheless installed by Someone.

Whom?

Why?

An act of Kindness?

Mercy?

Love?

A mystery?

Perhaps what I remember is a lie. Perhaps I just remember what I want. Perhaps I always knew the laws I fear.

When it lifts itself and with it, me, then am I raised and grateful so it seems.

I wonder if it's like the change in altitude in coming up from the ocean, from whence one never should have sunk, where life is neither meant to go, though if it does, ought to desist and not return, for if it does, it does diminished like that child I knew when I was young, who fell in the pool and almost drowned, who should have drowned but didn't, was rather "saved" to "live" in a coma on a diagonally slanted plank or "bed" in what was once the family living room, but then became, as it continues to be, the "treatment" room, yes, continues for she is still "living," now in her forties as she has been for the past three decades, breathing, receiving IV nourishment, evacuating, all with the assistance as she will for the rest of her miserable fucking "life" like a fucking vegetable while her poor pathetic delusional babbling mother, now some kind of religious nut, prays faithfully, still, after all these years, for pity's sake, for her little girl to recover while her husband, having not been able to stand the sight of his beloved daughter drooling her fucking life away, left, and honestly, who can blame the poor bastard, then only after years of serious boozing was finally able to off himself by, rumor has it, means involving a plastic bag, all the while nutty ol' Mom continues to pray, babble, and hope like crazy that her vegetable girl, excuse me, vegetable "woman," can still, yet, somehow against all reason, against all odds, against all that is decent, good, or right, by means, that is, of some dark miracle, recover.

Or if it is like the speed, as in a coming up from the ocean, something deeper than a merely nearly lethal suburban family swimming pool, too fast, from whence one never should have fallen, although one did, then being expelled, ejected, thrown, tossed, heaved, wretched up as in a vomiting forth, too rapidly, that makes one giddy, disoriented, distraught, and temporarily out of mind, temporarily buoyant as if shot through with hope, with light, or rather a thing mistaken for light, a flash or jolt or electrical event or something that induces or makes way for something else the name of which I cannot recall, the nature of which I cannot create, although the memory of which, because it is no more, although I so believed when I was young (I am no longer young), once seemed or was. Or if it is like nothing else at all.

There have been times when I've believed, when I have held belief as if it was a thing that I could hold. When I felt like I could feel the thing surrounding me and filling me and I became that thing and it was good.

Then I've been just the opposite.

Then everything, yes *every* particular, singular thing, both big and little, great and small, magnificent and miniscule, significant and meaningless, yes, every stupid trivial fucking thing was, is, as it was in the beginning is now and ever shall be without end, Amen, awful.

Then I am sunk have sunk I sink and all is sunk and dark and so am I. I no more nothing am, I am the worst, a stupid thing, a desperate thing who waits and fears some other thing will fall on her or flatten me, eviscerate or disembowel, or hook or crook or skewer me, or slam or knock me from behind, then kick me down and grind me in the gravel and remove the begging parts of me.

But I don't try to get away.

No, rather, I am begging, *Get me over with.*

When I consider how my life is spent.
My life is spent considering the ways.
Something . . . I . . . something? Let me count the ways:
The cliff, the car, the pill, the gun.
The breath that would be held for good.
The water, pool, the plastic bag.
The bottom of the ocean. That dark deep.

I care no more down with me whom I drag.

This hasn't always been the case. Maybe that has been another part of the problem: I have never been able to do things just for me. Especially if I thought what I did might affect someone else negatively. I didn't want to upset or hurt anyone (else). I was a good girl.

For example, for many years I said to myself: I can't do anything rash until Mom dies. I loved my mom and when she needed me to help her die, I did. But before she died I'd always thought I wouldn't be able, when push came to shove, to actually do my thing, because it would kill her, it would really kill her if I did something rash and I didn't want to hurt her. I didn't want her to die. Her life had been shitty enough without me giving her one more shitty thing to worry and feel truly shitty about: Why had I done it, what had gone wrong with me, could she have done anything to prevent it, etc., etc.

But then, after she died things were different.

But unfortunately not everything.

I wonder if the things I see when I am out of mind are things I'd not permit me to see otherwise.

I saw it otherwise when I was young.

But I can neither remember exactly nor entirely forget.

I tell myself I was because I want a former way to go back to.

I don't know where but somewhere, I desire to believe, of respite.

I have made the efforts. I have been valiant. I did the ridiculous assinine idiot things they recommended:

Do something nice for yourself! Get out into nature! Take a brisk walk to a beautiful park! Take up exercise, but don't be too hard on yourself! Start with a schedule you can stick to! Set a goal for yourself! But don't be too ambitious! Choose a goal you can achieve!

I got a kick out of that, "don't be too hard on yourself." I decided to try that one.

My exercise was this: I got out of bed. I unplugged the phone. I got back in bed.

Take a brisk walk to a beautiful park!

Attempting a "brisk" walk, neither then was I hard on myself. I shuffled. It was the first time I had been in something other than slippers or socks in I couldn't remember how long. (The sense of time was one of the first to go.) I went out "into nature."

I tried to think like that. I thought like this:

It's autumn! The leaves are changing! They're colorful! They're beautiful! They're red and yellow, oh let's call it gold! That sounds so festive! They're burnt and burnished brown—lovely! If only I were a painter! Or a photographer! If only—If only—

That was a bad idea. If only If only If only.

I couldn't do it. They may have been colorful, beautiful, and so forth, but fuck all if I could see like that.

I listened for the voices of the children. I had been told that they were lively, full of hope, the bright sounds of the future, and so forth, but sweet Jesus, give the poor little buggers a few years and they'll be singing a different tune.

I looked up at the sky. It looked like rain.

It is starting to rain. I know that soon enough, if not this time, the next, the heavens will open, the ocean will fall, and everything will be covered almost entirely again. Again I will be under where I always go, where every time I long for my release but neither stay down long enough nor do unto myself what I've been threatening, and promising, what I've been longing, begging, waiting to do for years, so I come back again.

For after a while it stops, it lifts.

Then after another while it will begin again.

Inheritance

I have his build, his coloring, his thick, brown, wavy hair. What finickiness I have is his, the way he washed his hands and clipped his nails. I have his temper and his obstinance, his tendency to brood. I get impatient like he did, I have his cruelty. I have his anger and his lust. I have, from him, the trouble I've had with booze.

From her I have my hands, my skin, the way she rocked back on her feet when she was nervous. I have her fear of walking on ice, her fear of being homeless. I talk to cats the way she did and coddle babies. I get the sudden, intense, almost ecstatic satisfaction she got from suddenly, obsessively cleaning house. I can carry a grudge the way she did and I remember slights. It takes me long, if not forever, to forgive.

One time, when I was in junior high, a while after my father had left, my mother suddenly yelled at me, "Stop it!! Stop!!" I looked at her like, "Wha—" She was flustered and apologized. But the way I was clipping my fingernails, she said, was exactly, "*exactly* the way your father did." She said it drove her crazy.

I have his love of music and I use it, like he did, to get away. I can, the way he did, shut people out. I can, the way he did, ignore someone who wants me. I can be repulsed by need.

I have her love of history, of guided tours with docents and of picnics in the cold. I learned, from her, to help old guys and ladies cross the street and to be patient with the crazies on the bus. I am, like her, afraid of drunks. And I have been, like him, a drunk.

I am like her, more happy eating cheap Chinese or Mexican food than in someplace that's "fancy." I get appalled, the way she did, what people pay for clothes, for food, for crap.

I want, like her, to not need anyone. I want, like him, to have someone always near. I fear, like her, that I will be betrayed. I fear I will, like him, betray whoever loves me. I fear I can't be trusted and I fear like him, that if I settle down, I will miss out on something grand.

I fear, how much, like both of them, I want. I fear that, like him, I will throw away my life. I fear, the way she did, that something awful will occur, a hurricane or earthquake and I will not be prepared and will lose everything.

I fear that there will never be enough. I fear I will be left by those I love.

Though both of them have been dead for years, I still get startled when I recognize some way I drop my hands or sink back on a couch or shake my head with disapproval at something on the news, and see anew exactly how I'm like them.

The way I suddenly go cold. The way I shut up midsentence, turn and walk away. The way I suddenly go off alone because I'm shaking, livid, angry, over something I won't say. The way I close the door so quietly when what I want to do is slam it.

The way I blame whoever's near me, or is absent, for my troubles. The way that I resent what I don't have. The way I feel that I deserve much more, and that I don't deserve my blessings. The way I want to be both left alone and to have someone follow me, pursue me, read my mind and heart and give me what I don't know how to ask. The way I would be loved entirely, though I cannot conceive of what that is.

Sometimes my spouse will say, when I have laughed or coughed or talked with the cats, "You sound just like your mother . . ." Or, when I think that someone's been incompetent — the postman delivering something late or the trainee at the counter who can't find my reservation — and I get arrogant and insulting and she says, "Well, I guess Dad's dropped in for a little visit . . ." I get angry at her for saying so, and am ashamed that she is right. I'm also, though, a bit relieved, as if my bad behavior's not my own, but what I have inherited, my disease.

When I'm afraid. When I can't stand. When I'm afraid to sleep.

I fear, as much as I desire, this inheritance.

I want to keep what they have given me, I want to rid myself of it.

I want to end the thing I am of them; I want them not to ever end.

There

What is no longer there. What was but is no more though you desire it. You recollect as if the calling back will bring it back, restoring it, the thing that still inheres that cannot be forgot nor lived without, the thing you try to say. The saying out is cry of loss, confession. It's regret. It's heaving up a fire you hope that someone else will see, a ghost or someone evil, big, above, who took, a flare in the dark that's recognized but not by them, but only by another, small, as small as you. You hope as if the recognition, spreading, will diminish what is yours, what is not bearable. But what cannot be borne cannot be lightened. What is uttered is not it, what you desire had not left. In one true way, it hasn't, but how it is still present is unbearable. And yet it will be borne. You bear it. The flare is a word, a cry, a longing to the other world, the longer one, the one away but better because it has the thing that left. But you are now in this world. You want to leave, you wish you could, and quietly, without a show, you'd be discreet except you can't. The world you would go to, you would leave, yes, everything, the body, air, except you can't, the body holds you here, is heaven. You do not ask to understand, you only want to end. You're willing to do the thing you must, to suffer. Because you cannot leave, you can't forget. But this world is no more enough. It never was although you didn't know before what now away from whence you cannot look. You write your letters to the dead. You say, Come back, come back. But they cannot. You say over and over and over again, as if they can, Come back, come back, come back, but they cannot.